# THE VAMPIRE WISH

DARK WORLD: THE VAMPIRE WISH 1

MICHELLE MADOW

DREAMSCAPE PUBLISHING

The Vampire Wish

Published by Dreamscape Publishing


ISBN: 9798406243077

THE DARK WORLD SERIES

**Dark World: The Vampire Wish**

The Vampire Wish

The Vampire Prince

The Vampire Trick

The Vampire Fate

The Vampire War

**Dark World: The Angel Trials**

The Angel Trials

The Angel Hunt

The Angel Trap

The Angel Gift

The Angel Island

The Angel Secret

The Angel Test

**Dark World: The Faerie Games**

The Faerie Games

The Faerie Pawn

The Faerie Mates

The Faerie Wand

The Faerie Plague

**Dark World: The Dragon Twins**

The Dragon Twins

The Dragon Realm

The Dragon Scorned

The Dragon Queen

# PROLOGUE: ANNIKA

"RACE YOU TO THE BOTTOM!" my older brother Grant yelled the moment we got off the chair lift.

Mom and Dad skied up ahead, but beyond the four of us, the rest of the mountain was empty. It was the final run of the trip, on our last day of winter break, and we'd decided to challenge ourselves by skiing down the hardest trail on the mountain—one of the double black diamond chutes in the back bowl.

The chutes were the only way down from where we were—the chairlift that took us up here specified that these trails were for experts only. Which was perfect for us. After all, I'd been skiing since I was four years old. My parents grew up skiing, and they couldn't wait to get me and Grant on the trails. We could tackle any trail at this ski resort.

"Did I hear something about a race?" Dad called from up ahead.

"Damn right you did!" Grant lifted one of his poles in the air and hooted, ready to go.

"You're on." I glided past all of them, the thrill of competition already racing through my veins.

Mom pleaded with us to be careful, and then my skis tipped over the top of the mountain, and I was flying down the trail.

I smiled as I took off. I'd always wanted to fly, but obviously that wasn't possible, and skiing was the closest thing I'd found to that. If I lived near a mountain instead of in South Florida, I might have devoted my extracurricular activities to skiing instead of gymnastics.

I blazed down the mountain like I was performing a choreographed dance, taking each jump with grace and digging my poles into the snow with each turn. This trail was full of moguls and even some rocky patches, but I flew down easily, avoiding each obstacle as it approached. I loved the rush of the wind on my cheeks and the breeze through my hair. If I held my poles in the air, it really *did* feel like flying.

I was lost in the moment—so lost that I didn't see the patch of rocks ahead until it was too late. I wasn't prepared for the jump, and instead of landing gracefully, I ploofed to the ground, wiping out so hard that both of my skis popped off of my boots.

"Wipeout!" Grant laughed, holding his poles up in the air and flying past me.

"Are you okay?" Mom asked from nearby.

"Yeah, I'm fine." I rolled over, locating my skis. One was next to me, the other a few feet above.

"Do you need help?" she asked.

"No." I shook my head, brushing the snow off my legs. "I've got this. Go on. I'll meet you all at the bottom."

She nodded and continued down the mountain, knowing me well enough to understand that I didn't need any help—I wanted to get back up on my own. "See you there!" she said, taking the turns slightly more cautiously than Grant and Dad.

I trudged up the mountain to grab the first ski, popped it back on, and glided on one foot to retrieve the other. I huffed as I prepared to put it back on. What an awful final run of the trip. My family was nearing the bottom of the trail—there was no way I would catch up with them now.

Looked like I would be placing last in our little race. Which annoyed me, because last place was *so* not my style.

But I still had to get down, so I took a deep breath, dug my poles into the snow, and set off.

As I was nearing the bottom, three men emerged from the forest near the end of the chute. None of them wore skis, and they were dressed in jeans, t-shirts, and leather jackets. They must have been freezing.

I stopped, about to call out and ask them if they needed help. Before I could speak, one of them moved in a blur, coming up behind my brother and sinking his teeth into his neck.

I screamed as Grant's blood gushed from the wound, staining the snow red.

The other two men moved just as fast, one of them pouncing on my mom, the other on my dad. More blood gushed from both of their necks, their bodies limp like rag dolls in their attackers arms.

"No!" I flew down the mountain—faster than I'd ever skied before—holding my poles out in front of me. I reached my brother first and jammed the pole into the back of his attacker with as much force as I could muster.

The pole bounced off the man, not even bothering him in the slightest, and the force of the attack pushed me to the ground. All I could do was look helplessly up as the man dropped my brother into the blood stained snow.

What was going on? Why were they *doing* this?

Then his gaze shifted to me, and he stared me down.

His eyes were hard and cold—and he snarled at me, baring his teeth.

They were covered in my brother's blood.

"Grant," I whispered my brother's name, barely able to speak. He was so pale—so still. And there was so much blood. The rivulets streamed from the puddles around him, the glistening redness so bright that it seemed fake against the frosty background.

One of the other men dropped my mom's body on the ground next to my brother. Seconds later, my dad landed next to them.

My mother's murderer grabbed the first man's shoulder—the man who had murdered my brother. "Hold it, Daniel," he said, stopping him from moving toward me.

I just watched them, speechless. My whole family was gone. These creatures ran faster than I could blink, and they were strong enough to handle bodies like they were weightless.

I had no chance at escape.

They were going to do this to me too, weren't they? These moments—right here, right now—would be my last.

I'd never given much thought to what happens after people die. Who does, at eighteen years old? I was supposed to have my whole life ahead of me.

My *family* was supposed to have their whole lives ahead of them, too.

Now their lifeless, bloody bodies at the bottom of this mountain would be the last things I would ever see.

I steadied myself, trying to prepare for what was coming. Would dying hurt? Would it be over quickly? Would I disappear completely once I was gone? Would my soul continue on, or would my existence be wiped from the universe forever?

It wasn't supposed to be this way. I didn't want to die. I wanted to *live.*

But I'd seen what those men—those *creatures*—had done to my family. And I knew, staring up at them, that it was over.

Terror filled my body, shaking me to the core. I couldn't fight them. I couldn't win. Against them, I was helpless.

And even if I stood a chance, did I really want to continue living while my family was gone?

"We can't kill them all," the man continued. "Laila sent us here to get humans to replace the ones that rabid vampire killed in his bloodlust rampage. We need to keep her alive."

"I suppose she'll do." The other man glared down at me, licking his lips and clenching his fists. "It's hard to tell under all that ski gear, but she looks pretty. She'll make a good addition to the Vale."

He took a syringe out of his jacket, ran at me in a blur, and jabbed the needle into my neck.

The empty, dead eyes of my parents were the last things I saw before my head hit the snow and everything went dark.

# 1

## ANNIKA

I HELD OUT MY ARM, watching as the needle sucked the blood from the crease of my elbow and into the clear vial. I sat there for ten minutes, staring blankly ahead as I did my monthly duty as a citizen of the Vale.

Like all humans who lived in the kingdom, I was required to donate blood once a month.

This was my twelfth time donating blood.

Twelve months. One year. That's how long it had been since my family had been murdered in front of my eyes and I'd been kidnapped to the Vale.

When I'd first been told that I was now a blood slave to vampires, I didn't believe it. Vampires were supposed to be *fiction*. They didn't exist in real life.

But I couldn't deny what I'd seen in front of my eyes. Those pale men, how quickly they'd moved, how they'd ripped their teeth into my parents and brother's throats and drained them dry, leaving their corpses at the bottom of that ski trail.

Why had I been the one chosen to live, and not them?

It was all because I'd fallen on that slope. If I hadn't fallen, I would have been first down the mountain. I would have been killed. My mom would have been last, and *she* would have been the one taken.

But my mom wouldn't have been strong enough to survive in the Vale. So even though I hated that I'd lived while they'd died, it was better that I lived in this hellish prison than any of them. I'd always been strong. Stubborn. Determined.

Those traits kept me going every day. They were the traits that kept me *alive*.

At first, I'd wanted to escape. I thought that if I could just get out of this cursed village, I could run to the nearest town and get help. I could save all the humans who were trapped in the Vale.

I didn't get far before a wolf tried to attack me.

I'd used my gymnastics skills to climb high up on a tree, but if Mike hadn't followed me, fought off the wolf, and dragged me back inside the Vale, I would have been dead meat. The wolves would have eventually gotten to me and feasted upon my body, leaving nothing but bones.

Mike had told me everything about the wolves as we'd walked back to the Tavern. He'd grown up in the Vale, so he knew a lot about its history. He'd told me that they weren't regular wolves—they were shifters. They'd made a pact with the vampires centuries ago, after the vampires had invaded their land and claimed this valley as their own. He'd told me about how the wolves craved human flesh as much as the vampires craved human blood, and how if a human tried to escape—if they crossed the line of the Vale—they became dinner to the wolves.

At least the vampires let us live, so they could have a continuous supply of blood to feast upon whenever they wanted.

The wolves just killed on the spot.

That was the first and last time I'd tried to escape. And after Mike had saved me, we'd become best friends. He'd offered me my job at the Tavern, where I'd been working—and living—ever since. All of us who worked there lived in the small rooms above the bar, sleeping in the bunks inside.

He and the others had helped me cope with the transition—with realizing I was a slave to the vampires, and that as a mere human amongst supernaturals, there was no way out.

They were my family now.

"You're done," the nurse said, removing the needle

from my arm. She placed a Band-Aid on the bleeding dot, and I flexed my elbow, trying to get some feeling back in the area. "See you next month."

"Yeah." I gathered my bag and stood up. "Bye."

On my way out, I passed Martha—the youngest girl who worked at the Tavern. She slept in the bunk above mine, and along with being the youngest, she was also the smallest.

It took her twice as long to recover from the blood loss as it did for me.

"Good luck," I told her on the way out. "I'll see you back at the Tavern." I winked, and she smiled, since she knew what I was about to do.

It was what I always did on blood donation day.

I held my bag tightly to my side and stepped onto the street, taking a deep breath of the cold mountain air. It was dark—us humans were forced to adjust to the vampires' nocturnal schedule—and I could see my breath in front of me. The witch who'd created the shield to keep the Vale hidden from human eyes also regulated the temperature, but she could only do so much. And since it was December in Canada, it was naturally still cold.

I hurried to the busiest street in town—Main Street, as it was so creatively named. Humans manned stalls, and vampires walked around, purchasing luxuries that only they were afforded. Meat, doughnuts, pizza, cheeses—you name it, the vampires bought it.

The vampires didn't even *need* food to survive, but they ate it anyway, because it tasted good.

Us humans, on the other hand, were relegated to porridge, bread, rice, and beans—the bare necessities. The vampires thought of us as nothing but cattle—as blood banks. And blood banks didn't deserve food for enjoyment. Only for nourishment.

Luckily, Mike had taught me a trick or two since the day he'd saved me from the wolves. After seeing me climb that tree, he'd called me "scrappy" and said it was a skill that would get me far in the Vale.

He'd taught me how to steal.

It was ironic, really. Stealing hadn't been something that had ever crossed my mind in my former life. I used to have it good—successful, loving parents, trips to the Caribbean in the winter, skiing out west in the spring, and an occasional voyage to Europe thrown in during the summers. I'd had a credit card, and when I'd needed something, I would buy it without a second thought.

I hadn't appreciated how good I'd had it until all of that was snatched away and I was left with nothing.

Now I walked past the various booths, eyeing up the delicious food I wasn't allowed to have. But more than the food, I was eying up the shopkeepers and the vampires around them. Who seemed most oblivious? Or absorbed in conversation?

It didn't take long to spot a vampire woman flirting with a handsome human shopkeeper. I'd seen enough of vampires as a species to know that if the flirting was going to progress anywhere, it would lead to him becoming one of her personal blood slaves, but he followed her every movement, entranced by her attention.

They were the only two people at the booth. Everyone else was going about their own business, not paying any attention to me—the small, orphaned blood slave with downcast eyes and torn up jeans.

Which gave me the perfect opportunity to snatch the food that us humans were forbidden to purchase.

# 2

## ANNIKA

I PRESSED up against the stall, brushed a pile of candies into my bag, and scurried away.

Not bothering to glance behind, I stayed to the side of the street, scuttled through an alley, and passed through to the other side. Once there, I leaned against the wall, finally able to breathe again.

Every time I stole, I feared getting caught.

But that wouldn't stop me from doing it. After all, this was the only revenge I had against the vampires. They might have taken away my family, and they might have taken away my freedom, but I refused to let them take away my dignity.

As a human, I was weak and they were strong. I hated them for it, but at the same time, I *envied* them for it. Because after they'd murdered my family in front of my eyes and I was powerless to stop it, I never wanted to feel that helpless again.

But I *did* feel helpless. Every day since I was taken here. How could I not, as a human amongst such powerful creatures? To them, we were animals. We were slaves.

I wish I had the power to change that.

For now, all I had was the power to take from them. Small things, and they never even noticed, but it was the only revenge I had.

I leaned against the wall and smiled, since once again, I'd gotten away with it. And so, after taking a few more deep breaths and steadying the pounding of my heart, I turned the corner and approached the bookstore.

It was empty inside besides the owner, Norbert. He sat at his desk, his eyeglasses on as he read a book. He was an older man—I always imagined that if we weren't prisoners in the Vale, he would have been a professor at some fancy college. Perhaps even a college I might have chosen to attend.

The moment the door closed, he looked up and smiled at me. "Annika," he said, placing his glasses down at the table. "Anything specific you're looking for today?"

"Just browsing," I told him. "Have you gotten in a new shipment yet?"

"It's only been a few days!" He laughed and leaned back in his chair. "I swear, you read faster than new books can arrive."

"I'm sure I can find something I missed before." I smiled and made my way over to my favorite shelf—the fantasy section—and got started on examining the spines, pulling out the titles that looked interesting and reading the back covers.

Before coming to the Vale, I hadn't been much of a reader—at least, I'd never read books that weren't assigned for class. Between school, gymnastics practices, homework, and spending time with my friends, I didn't have time to read for fun. If I needed to relax after a long day, I usually went straight to the television.

But us humans in the Vale didn't have access to televisions—or to the internet at all. And even with my work at the Tavern, now that I was no longer training for gymnastics competitions I had a lot more extra time on my hands. So I'd discovered the one pastime that humans in the Vale *were* allowed—books.

The books I found at the store here were much more to my taste than the books I'd been assigned to read at school. It hadn't been long until I'd discovered that I loved getting lost in the lives and stories of other people. I loved exploring their hardships, their trials, their love, and how they overcame most everything, despite what seemed like impossible odds.

These days, books were the only things that gave me hope. I treasured them and the stories within them more than anything else in the world.

"That'll be five coins," Norbert said once I placed the book I'd chosen on the counter.

"I don't have coins," I told him. "But I do have something I can trade."

He watched me, waiting, and I pulled one of the candy bars out of my bag. His eyes widened, and he leaned forward with such enthusiasm that I imagined he could practically taste the chocolate already.

It worked every time.

"You're going to get yourself in some serious trouble one day," he said, his eyes full of warning.

"Perhaps. But that doesn't stop you from enjoying the candy," I teased. "So… are you willing to trade, or not?"

"You know I am." He smiled, and as he passed me the book, I handed him the chocolate.

I pulled the book to my chest to give it a small hug, placed it in my bag with the rest of the candies, and headed back to the Tavern.

# 3

# JACEN

THE SCREAMS. The hunger. The blood.

I'd never forget the terrified looks on each of my victim's faces as I'd sunk my fangs into their necks and drained the lives from their bodies.

They haunted my dreams since the massacre. I relived it every night. The lust for their blood—the scent of it so tantalizingly delicious that my entire body burned for it, my fangs pushing through my gums and craving the silky feeling of the warm, smooth blood flowing down my throat. The way my soul parted with my mind as it gave into the craving—the desire for more and more until I'd consumed so much blood that every inch of my body was bloated and bursting with it.

It had been nearly a year since the massacre, and the

nightmares hadn't stopped. I didn't think they ever would.

I would never forgive myself for the pain and heartbreak I'd caused that night when I lost control of my bloodlust and slaughtered those humans in the village. So many of them had died that Queen Laila had to send out troops to replenish their stock.

*Stock.* As if they were crates of meat, or animals waiting to be slaughtered.

In my dreams, I saw the face of my final victim—the young boy who must have been no older than twelve. Then I woke up with a sharp breath, my fangs out and my gums aching for blood.

As always, a glass of it waited on my nightstand.

I reached for it, downing it in nearly one gulp. It tasted bitter—refrigerated blood always did—but it satisfied the craving enough that after a few deep breaths, I was able to pull my fangs back up into my gums and keep them there.

Still, my body craved more. But I didn't *need* more—I just *wanted* it. The craving was in my mind. It was an addiction—it wasn't real. What I'd just consumed was enough to sustain me for the rest of the day.

The blood I craved was my greatest desire and my greatest enemy.

After first turning, the lust for it controlled my every thought. But as the days had passed—slowly but surely—I'd improved at controlling my cravings. Three glasses in the morning eventually became two, and then became one.

Still, Laila refused to let me leave the palace. Not until I could prove that I could control my bloodlust around humans. After all, she couldn't have me killing any more of them. Not after the *inconvenience* I'd caused a year ago when I'd lost myself to that bloodlust filled haze.

Never mind the *inconvenience* she'd caused me by turning me into a vampire against my will.

And while I was strong, I wasn't strong enough to take down a group of guards on my own.

It was hard to believe it had only been a year ago that I'd been a human, unaware of the existence of supernaturals at all. After being locked in this palace for all that time, that year felt like an eternity.

This extravagant palace hidden in the wilderness of the Canadian Rockies—in an enchanted valley that the vampires called the Vale—had become my prison. Every day, I was suffocating. I needed to get out.

Which was why I'd been working daily on controlling my bloodlust. And slowly but surely, I'd been getting better.

Now, I placed the glass down on my nightstand and looked out my window as the last rays of the sun sunk over the horizon. I took deep, measured breaths, and the craving disappeared, my veins cooling down entirely.

I smiled, knowing this was it. I was ready to prove that I'd gained control of the monstrous creature I'd become.

I was ready to be free.

# 4

## JACEN

"Your Highness," my vampire guard Daniel said as he stepped inside my room.

I didn't think I would ever get used to being called that. After all, I was no prince. As a human, I'd been an eager swimmer, ready to conquer my first Olympics and get gold medals in as many categories as possible.

That person had died the moment Laila sank her fangs into my neck and damned me to an eternity of hell.

Daniel glanced at the empty glass on my nightstand, no hint of emotion flickering across his eyes. "Would you like another glass of blood?" he asked.

"No." I walked over to the window, observing the nearby village. Lights were starting to flicker on in the small houses the humans lived in. Just as I, they were preparing to start their day. Well, *night*, since we operated on a nocturnal schedule in the Vale.

I turned back to face Daniel. "I would like to speak with Queen Laila," I said.

He pressed his lips together, saying nothing. "Is it an important matter?" he finally asked. "As you know, the queen just returned from visiting the Carpathian Kingdom, and she has to catch up on everything she missed in her absence."

"It's important." I held his gaze and flexed my arms by my sides. "I'm ready."

"For what?" he asked.

"To put myself in the presence of a human."

---

Laila entered my room thirty minutes later, her trusted witch advisor Camelia following obediently behind her.

Camelia, as always, wore a glass pendant around her neck with a piece of wormwood inside. As a witch, she was one of the only mortals in the kingdom allowed to use wormwood to protect herself. Laila wore a short, flowing blue dress, and her raven colored hair flowed behind her, making her look more like a teen Hollywood starlet than a centuries year old monster.

She was the worst kind of monster—the kind you never saw coming.

I sure hadn't.

On the night I'd met her in a bar, all I was thinking was that she was a beautiful girl, and that I wanted nothing more than to bring her back to my hotel room and see how far she was willing to go with me.

If someone had told me what she *really* was, I would have laughed in their face.

Because Laila wasn't just an ordinary vampire. She was one of the *original* vampires.

There had been seven of them in all. All part of a cult of witches who were so determined to stay young and beautiful forever that they'd created a spell using dark magic to make them exactly what they'd wanted—immortal.

None of them knew it would turn them into monsters. At least, that's what the six living originals claimed.

But I didn't believe it. Because none of them seemed to hate what they were. In fact, they seemed to *relish* in it.

"Jacen," Laila said my name, the slight lilt in her accent the only evidence that she wasn't from this place and time. "Are you sure you're ready?"

"Especially after what happened last time," Camelia added with a smirk.

As always, the green-eyed witch loved to taunt me. I knew she was referring to four months ago—the last time I tried to drink from a human. They hadn't been able to bring him through the door before I'd caught a whiff of his scent and lost myself to the haze of my bloodlust.

The next thing I'd known, I was staring at his corpse on the ground, the last bits of his blood dripping off my fangs and onto the polished marble floor by my feet.

"I suppose the loss of one human won't be too big of a deal." Camelia waved her hand and turned to Laila. "But of course, the decision is yours, Your Highness."

Laila eyed me up thoughtfully, tilting her head and softly biting her blood red lip. "The loss of one human would be irrelevant," she confirmed. "Daniel—go fetch one from the dungeons. An old one, who wouldn't be much use to us anyway."

Daniel rushed out of the room in a blur, returning ten minutes later dragging a thin, older man with a chain. "Sit," he commanded the man, throwing him onto the nearest armchair.

The man cowered in the chair and curled up into a ball, shaking and not looking up at any of us.

I smelled his blood—the rich, thick liquid pulsing through his veins, and it was so tempting that my fangs itched to protrude. His jugular pulsed and pulsed, calling me closer.

But I swallowed down the urge, forcing my breaths

to become shallow. I could control myself. I *had* to control myself.

It was the only way to prove that I was able to leave the palace.

"Very good." Laila nodded after a full minute had passed.

"That's it?" I asked her. "Are we done here?"

"No." She pressed her lips together, mischief dancing in her bright blue eyes. "You've only proven that you can be *around* a human."

"Isn't that what I needed to prove?" I asked. "That I can be around them without losing control?"

"You're a vampire prince." She ran a finger along one of my arms and pulled away, smiling sinfully. "Your stamina needs to be stronger than that."

"How so?" I clenched my fists tighter, ignoring her touch. Instead, I stared at the man's neck again, dreading her next words.

"I want you to drink from him."

## 5

## JACEN

"You want me to kill him?" I kept my gaze on hers, unwilling to look at the human in question.

"No." The smug smile remained on her deceivingly innocent face. "I want you to drink from him and to control yourself. I want you to pull away *before* killing him. To enjoy your meal and leave him alive."

"I don't think I can do that." I stared her down, since she must know I was right. She was asking me to do this because she wanted me to kill him.

I shouldn't have expected anything less from her.

The vampire queen *looked* young and innocent, but her soul was dark and twisted.

"You can do it," she said simply. "As a great scientist once said—if you put your mind to it, you can accomplish anything."

"That's not a real scientist." I glared at her. "It's a quote from a movie."

"That's irrelevant." She waved my point away. "The point is that it's the truth. You're a vampire now, Jacen. The strongest of all species."

Camelia gave a small huff, but Laila ignored her.

"When I turned you last year, I gave you a gift," Laila continued.

"A gift I never wanted."

"Nevertheless, I gave it to you," she said. "You're a vampire prince now, Jacen. Show me that you deserve the title."

"And if I don't?" I challenged.

"You do." She laughed, light and melodic. "You may not see it now, but you will. Someday, you will. But for now—feed from him."

I eyed up the human man. How did he get in the prison? How old was he? Did he have a family?

I couldn't ask in front of Laila and Camelia. They viewed the human blood slaves as animals instead of people. Angering them would get me nowhere.

Instead, I created answers to the questions to myself. I imagined that this man had a family—a newborn grandchild he was excited to get to know. That he wanted his family to have more food than their rations allowed, since the rations only afforded bare survival for the humans. So he stole—bread from the vampires. The bread that vampires didn't even *need* to eat to survive, but enjoyed anyway, simply because they could. He got caught, and was unfairly locked in the dungeons, doomed to become a personal blood slave for the vampires in the palace—doomed to have them drink and drink from him until he died of blood loss and his remains were fed to the wolves outside the enchanted boundaries.

I looked into his eyes, trying to convince myself that this story I'd created for him was true.

Humanizing him might be the difference between if I was able to stop myself from losing myself to the bloodlust or if I killed him.

"Are you ready?" Laila sighed and tapped her foot impatiently. "We don't have all day."

"I'm ready." I stared at the man—examining his wrinkled face and reminding myself of the story I'd created.

I wouldn't kill him.

I would let him live.

I inched toward him and lowered myself down, my fangs sliding out of my gums as the scent of his blood filled my nose. Then my teeth sunk into his flesh and I was gulping down the warm, fresh blood.

How had I thought that the bitter, refrigerated blood could compare? How had I convinced myself that I could live off that garbage for the rest of my immortal existence? Noble vampires in the Vale were afforded the luxury of drinking straight from humans—I should *enjoy* the indulgence, not cower away from it.

It wasn't like I had much else to look forward to anymore. Not after my mortal life—my *soul*—had been taken from me against my will.

If the intoxicating taste of fresh blood was all I could enjoy, then so be it.

Just when I was beginning to enjoy myself, the blood supply stopped. I sucked deeper on his neck, trying to will out the final drops, and I squeezed his arms harder, as if that could push out more blood.

But there was nothing left.

He was drained dry.

# 6

# CAMELIA

I LOVED WATCHING JACEN FEED.

Ever since he'd been brought to the palace, I'd been fascinated by the vampire prince—the handsome swimmer I'd advised that Laila turn after her previous prince had been driven mad by the bloodlust and had sacrificed himself to the wolves.

As Jacen drained the old man, I reached for the pendant I always wore around my neck—the one filled with wormwood—stroking it and holding my breath. I watched as the man stopped struggling, as his hands went limp, and as his head eventually rolled to the side, his eyes empty and dead.

As predicted, Jacen had lost control again. Consumed by his bloodlust. It wasn't surprising.

Because the stronger the vampire, the harder it was for them to control their urge to drain humans dry.

Jacen was shaping up to become one of the most powerful vampires that ever existed.

And I was determined to make him mine.

"Take the body away," Laila told Daniel, barely glancing at the drained corpse.

Jacen didn't tear his eyes away from the old man as Daniel heaved him over his shoulder and walked out of the room.

"You're not ready," Laila told Jacen sharply. "In time you will be, but not yet."

"How do I control it?" he asked her—begged her. "Why don't I know when to stop?"

"You're improving," Laila said. "The fact that you didn't maul him the moment you smelled his blood was significant progress. But you need more time."

"How much more?"

"There's no exact formula," she said. "It will happen when you want it badly enough. In the meantime, I have work to attend to."

She exited the room, leaving Jacen and me alone.

"What are you staring at?" he growled at me. "Don't you have work to do, too? A kingdom to help Laila run?"

"Of course." I nodded. "But I also wanted to let you know that I'm here for you, if you ever want to talk."

"Don't play that game with me." He scowled.

"What game?" I reached for the amulet again, forming my expression into one that I hoped looked like complete innocence.

"The game where you pretend to care about anyone except for yourself."

"There's no pretense here," I told him. "I *do* care about you. I want you to become the strongest vampire prince that ever lived. Perhaps even a king."

"I'll never become a king." He crossed his arms. "I don't *want* to become a king."

"Then what do you want?" I asked, truly curious.

"To be human again."

"Why?" I laughed. "Even if that were possible—which it isn't—why would you refuse the power you've been given? Why would you want to be so weak?"

"I'm not going to bother explaining it to you." He looked away from me and walked over to the window, gazing longingly at the human village below. "You'll never understand."

"I might understand more than you think." I slithered toward him, and when I was close enough, I laid my hand gently on his shoulder. "I understand that you need comfort, Jacen. I can provide that. Let me give it to you."

I leaned forward, looking deep into his eyes, my lips getting closer and closer to his. What would kissing him feel like? I imagined that old man's blood must still coat his tongue—I wished I could know how delicious it tasted to him.

It must have been incredible, to make him lose control like he did.

"Stop." He stepped back, his eyes dilating as he stared into mine. "Leave my quarters. Now."

"Are you trying to compel me?" I laughed again, although disappointment fluttered in my stomach. I wouldn't be turned away that easily. Instead, I leaned forward again, willing him to give into temptation. He'd given in with that human. Why not with me?

He simply backed away and repeated his command.

"You know I'm wearing wormwood," I continued, reaching for my necklace. "Your compulsion won't work on me."

Compulsion was an ability that only the originals—and the vampires they directly turned—possessed. It was the ability to make others do as they willed. It could be used to achieve greatness, but it could also be used to achieve great destruction. Which was why the originals were extremely selective in who they turned into a vampire prince or princess.

They couldn't risk creating a vampire who might use the powers they'd been gifted to destroy their own sire.

"We're done here." He took another step away from

me, narrowing his eyes. "Unless you have anything more you need to say?"

"No," I said. "At least, not now."

With that, I turned on my heel and headed out the door. Fire ran through my veins as I stomped down the hall—frustration. I hated not getting what I wanted.

Jacen may not want me now. But in time, he would learn to.

Because eventually, I would be his queen.

## 7

# CAMELIA

"CAMELIA." Laila closed her laptop, pushed it aside, and laced her hands together on top of her desk. "I heard you wanted to discuss something with me in private?"

"Yes." I nodded. "I want to talk to you about Jacen."

"What about him?" She leaned back in her chair, raising an eyebrow.

"He's getting better and better at controlling his bloodlust each day." I stood calm and steady, making sure not to twist my hands together or do anything else that might give away the anxiety catapulting through my veins. "Technically, he could even leave the palace, since he's able to be around humans without attacking them."

"I agree that he's able to leave the palace," Laila said. "But he's a prince—and a powerful one, at that. If he wanted to leave the palace walls, it's up to him to trust himself and seize the opportunity."

"So you're testing him?" I smirked, since it was so like Laila to do such a thing.

"I'm testing *everyone*," she said. "All the time. Never forget that."

"I won't," I promised, using every ounce of willpower to keep the irritation from my tone. As long as Laila lived, this was her kingdom, and I had to play by her rules.

For now.

"Anyway," she continued. "Is that all you wanted to tell me? That you think Jacen is ready to have freedom to roam outside the palace?"

"No," I stuttered, and then I cleared my throat, composing myself. If I wanted Laila to consider my request, I had to be as royal as possible. "I'm here because I agree that Jacen has the potential to be a powerful vampire prince. But I believe he'll be stronger with an equally powerful woman by his side."

Laila tilted her head and smiled in a way that made me think she already knew what was coming. "What are you proposing?" she asked.

"I would like to be betrothed to Jacen," I said. "With the two of us united as prince and princess of the Vale, the kingdom will become stronger than ever."

Laila was quiet for a few seconds, and I resisted the

urge to fidget. She was sizing me up—I knew it. I had to prove that I was the proper match for Jacen.

After all, if Laila declared our betrothal, he would have no choice but to accept me—to learn to love me.

Given time, he *would* learn to love me. I would make sure of it.

"The two of you would be a strong pair," Laila finally said, and with that admission, I could finally breathe again. "But you do realize what a union between the two of you would mean?"

"Are you referring to the fact that I would need to become a vampire?" I asked.

"Yes." She nodded. "And, like all witches who become vampires, once the transformation is complete you will lose your ability to perform magic."

"I'm aware," I told her. "But while I'll lose my magic, I'll become immortal and gain the strength of a vampire. It's a trade I'm happy to make. It's a trade I *want* to make."

"You've given this much thought," she stated, and I nodded, since I had. "I agree that you would take well to being a vampire. I would even change you myself."

"Thank you, my queen," I said, lowering myself into a curtsy. "That would be the greatest honor. I would be forever in your debt."

She held a hand up, stopping me. "But there is a condition."

"What kind of condition?" I faltered.

"You know as well as I that witches—especially witches with powers like yours—are rare," she said.

I nodded again, since this was common knowledge. Centuries after the original vampires had come into existence, they'd become such a plague upon humanity that the angels in Heaven had come down to Earth to give birth to a new race of creatures—the Nephilim. Or hunters, as our kind preferred to call them. The purpose of the Nephilim had been to protect humanity by ridding the world of vampires. They'd killed Laila's sister—one of the seven original vampires—and the six remaining originals had fled to the different continents. With the help of a few witches, they'd gone into hiding, to the locations that had later become the six vampire kingdoms. Vampires either joined the kingdoms, or were killed by hunters. Rogue vampires rarely lasted long in the wild before being hunted down and killed.

Then, a few decades ago, the most powerful witch in the world had been born—Geneva. It was rumored that there was no spell she couldn't do—that she could grant any wish desired. As what usually happens to those with great power, she was revered, but also feared. When the Nephilim had gotten word of her powers, they'd changed their mission from not just hunting vampires, but to hunting witches as well.

The majority of the witch population had been slain in the years that followed.

It had looked like the Nephilim were going to win. But the six vampire kingdoms and the witches had banded together, even bringing the wolves to their side. In the Great War that had followed, the three supernatural races managed to work together and rid the world of the Nephilim forever.

But like most wars, there had been many casualties. That was why not many witches remained today.

It was why I was so valuable to the Vale.

"You will need to find a suitable witch to replace you," Laila said.

"Do you have anyone in mind?" I asked. "I'm sure if I approached them, they would be thrilled to have the job."

"I do." Laila twirled a strand of hair around her finger, her eyes slanted with mischief. "As I'm sure you know, the wolves have been becoming… less and less cooperative as of late. Just last week, one of them broke through the boundary and had that old lady for lunch."

"That wolf was killed for her actions," I reminded Laila. "The treaty has existed for centuries. The wolves know their place."

"They did," Laila said. "But they've been getting restless. This land was originally theirs, and now that we've turned it into a thriving kingdom, they're jealous. They want it back. I suspect it won't be long until the problem escalates into something we won't be able to hide from the public any longer."

"And you need a witch to keep them in control," I said, since wolves tended to respect witches more than vampires. Likely because both witches and wolves were natural creatures, whereas vampires were created by a spell.

"Not just any witch," Laila said. "I want Geneva."

"Geneva?" I repeated, my eyes wide. "But that... that's impossible."

"It's not impossible," Laila said. "Just highly difficult. And I would hope that you—as someone who claims to be worthy of being betrothed to Jacen—are up to the task."

I watched her, dumbfounded, waiting for her to say that this was some kind of joke.

She just stared at me, waiting.

I couldn't believe this.

Because Geneva had survived the Great War—her powers had been hugely helpful in winning. But after a few years, she'd grown restless. She'd wanted to do *more* with her powers. And she'd become convinced that she could perfect the immortality spell—the spell the original vampires had performed on themselves when they were witches. The spell that had gone wrong and made them dependent on the blood of humans for the rest of their immortal lives.

She was going to perform the spell on herself.

The witches wouldn't hear of it. Geneva was powerful, yes, but what if the spell went wrong? What if it resulted in something worse than vampires? Or what if it made her more powerful than she already was?

It was far too risky.

And so, the witches had banded together. They'd used their powers to lock Geneva's spirit inside a powerful stone. A sapphire ring. Then they'd hidden the ring in a place that no human could find, and that couldn't be accessed by any magical creature that existed on Earth. It was called the Crystal Cavern, and many other magical objects that posed too much of a threat to the lives of all creatures on Earth had been stowed there as well. Throughout the years, some darker witches had tried to lead humans there to fetch the objects, but all of the humans had ended up dead.

"The Crystal Cavern doesn't allow supernaturals inside," I reminded Laila. "And it kills the humans who enter."

"There has to be a loophole," Laila said, tapping her pen on her desk. "I was a witch once. If there's one thing I know about spells, it's that there's always a loophole."

"Perhaps if we found an exceptionally strong

human," I suggested. "They might be able to fight whatever's guarding the objects inside the cavern and retrieve the ring."

"That sounds like a good plan." Laila nodded. "Although you will be the one in charge of finding the human—not me. I trust this is something you can handle?"

"Yes." I swallowed, wishing I could feel as confident as I sounded.

"Excellent." Laila smiled and placed her hands on her desk. "Now, be on your way. And the next time you come to me, I hope it's to re-introduce me to my old friend Geneva."

# 8

# JACEN

I AWOKE as the last rays of the sun set below the horizon, opening my eyes to see someone standing next to my bed—Laila.

"Good evening," she said, dangling a glass of blood in front of my face. Unlike the refrigerated blood I kept on my nightstand, this blood was warm—fresh.

I went to take it from her, but she held it out of my reach and backed away. She watched me, her eyes full of challenge, and she took a deep breath and smiled, as if enjoying the fragrance of the blood.

"Did you come in here to tease me?" The scent of the blood filled my nose, my mouth watering as my fangs pressed against my gums. I wanted nothing more than to yank that blood out of Laila's hand and pour the blood down my throat.

But Laila was the queen, and it was up to her to decide when I would be free of the palace. She was testing me—I knew it.

I forced my breathing to become shallow so I wouldn't have to inhale the intoxicating scent of the blood. Every bone in my body itched to run for the glass, but I pushed the urge down. I had to control myself. I have to *prove* myself.

"Well?" I asked once I'd regained control, making sure to look at Laila's face and not at the tempting glass of liquid in her hand.

"I came in here to talk to you." She stepped closer and handed me the glass.

I took it from her and finished it in a few gulps.

She watched me the entire time, her face a mask hiding whatever thoughts or emotions might be flying through her mind.

"How have you been feeling each evening upon waking?" she asked, perching on the side of my bed.

"Hungry," I said, since it was the truth.

"But the hunger has been improving since you were first turned, has it not?"

"It hasn't," I said. "But my control over it has."

"I see that." She glanced approvingly at the now empty glass. "You wouldn't have been able to resist that blood even a week ago."

"I've been practicing."

"Very good." She smirked, and I had a feeling that whatever she wanted to talk to me about, I wasn't going to like it. "Because I have a proposal for you—one that won't just be good for you, but will benefit the entire kingdom."

I stilled, getting the feeling that this might be trouble. "I'm listening," I said.

"Good." She laughed. "Because now that you're gaining control over your bloodlust, there's something important we need to discuss."

"The removal of my guards so I'll be able to leave the palace?" I guessed, hoping she would take it as a suggestion and agree.

"Nope." She smiled again. "Your guards will not be removed. No—what I want to discuss is *much* more exciting than that."

"And what is that?" I asked, since she was clearly goading me, and it would be much more efficient to simply say what she wanted so she would spill.

"It's time for you to start searching for a bride."

## 9

## JACEN

"WHAT?" I stared at her with wide eyes, running a hand through my hair. "You've got to be kidding me. No way."

"I can assure you that I'm not 'kidding you,'" she said. "I'm completely serious."

"I was turned into a vampire against my will," I reminded her. "And now you want me to marry against my will? Like I said—no way. I'm drawing the line with this request."

"What do you have against marriage?" she asked.

"Nothing," I said. "I have nothing against marriage—once I've fallen in love and decided I'm ready for it."

"You're a prince, my son," she said, brushing her finger across my cheek. It took all of my willpower not to flinch away. "Princes don't always have the luxury of marrying for love."

"If you're so desperate for a wedding around here, why don't *you* get married?" I threw at her. "You've been around for a few centuries. Surely you know someone you would want to wed?"

She glanced down at her hands, sadness crossing over her eyes—a rare moment of emotion for Laila. "There's only one person in the world I would marry, and that person is gone," she said softly. Then she yanked her head back up, her eyes hard and stubborn, all traces of sadness gone. "Besides, I am an *original* vampire. I am the queen of this kingdom. It is *you* who will be stronger with a match—not I. And I have the perfect match planned for you."

"Really?" I tried my best to sound bored, although my heart leapt into my throat with panic. "And who's that?"

"Camelia."

"What?" I backed up, horror rushing through my body. "No. *Hell* no. I'm *not* marrying that witch."

"Why not?" Laila asked. "Camelia proposed the idea herself, and I think it's a wonderful match. After all, you know that Camelia is a distant relative of mine—a descendant of my sister who was killed by the Nephilim. She has the bloodline to become a vampire princess—and she's willing to turn. I don't understand what the problem is."

"Centuries of being alive, and you don't understand what the problem is?" I glared at her, figuring she must be joking. But she watched me, waiting for me to continue, so I did. "The problem is that I don't love her."

"Love." Laila scrunched her nose. "Highly overrated, if you ask me. True love is rare, and only comes around once in a lifetime, if ever. Then once you find it, it has the power to break you. It's not worth the heartache. Trust me on that."

I shook my head, unwilling to believe her. I'd always thought that someday, I would meet the love of my life. Get married. Have children. The whole nine yards.

Of course, as a vampire, children were impossible. Unless I decided to turn someone and become their sire, which wasn't quite the same, and besides, I wouldn't wish this life as a monster on anyone.

But love was possible as a vampire. Many of the vampires I'd seen around the palace had chosen mates. They seemed happy together. They seemed in love.

"Good thing I'm immortal, then," I said, matching her smirk with my own. "With a longer life, I'll have much better odds at finding love. Don't you think?"

"Such hope." Laila sighed and ran her hand through her hair. "I'm so used to talking to immortals who look young, that sometimes I forget you actually *are* the age you appear. But when you're immortal, even if you find love, it will only destroy you in the end. I wouldn't wish that pain on anyone. But…" she continued. "I do have another proposal for you."

I resisted rolling my eyes. Because of *course* there was something else Laila wanted.

"And what's that?" I asked, since she was going to tell me if I asked or not.

"If you refuse to accept Camelia, then I'll provide you one year to find an alternate bride," she said. "You can choose from the vampire princesses in any of the other five kingdoms."

"Only from the other five?" I asked. "Not from the Vale?"

"This match will strengthen our alliance with one of the other kingdoms." Laila watched me, her head tilted in curiosity. "Now, do you have any more questions?"

"A few," I said. "Starting with—why are you so eager to have me marry within a year? As you said, we're immortal. Why the rush?"

"Good question." She nodded. "I haven't spoken to anyone except a handful of guards about this issue, so I expect you'll remain quiet about it, but the wolves are starting to resist our control. Just last week, one managed to cross the border of the Vale and feasted on an old woman who lived in the outskirts of the village."

"Isn't that against the treaty with them?" I asked.

"It is," she said. "But the wolves are multiplying quickly, and I believe it won't be long until they rebel and try to take our land. So we have two options. The first is to go out into the world and find more humans to turn so that we have more vampire soldiers. But that could get messy, since it's unpredictable how new vampires will react to the bloodlust."

I nodded, remembering an event that had happened recently—a newly turned vampire who had been brought into the palace. She'd been so distraught about what she was, and so unable to handle the bloodlust, that she'd rammed a silver stake straight into her heart.

I didn't know an exact percentage of how many newly turned vampires lost their minds to the change, but it happened more often than not.

Most humans couldn't handle being turned into a monster.

"So you want to strengthen an alliance so we can work together to fight the wolves," I realized. "Put them back into their place so they're no longer a threat."

"Smart boy," she said. "I knew there was a reason why I turned you."

"It makes sense," I said, since it did. "But why me? Why not Stephenie?" I asked, referring to the vampire "sister" I still barely knew. She was too interested in jet setting with her friends or leading on her latest boy-toy to pay a newly turned prince any attention.

"According to our traditions, if Stephenie marries a vampire prince from another kingdom, she'll move there to live with them," Laila explained. "However, if you marry, your bride will come here, and her kingdom —whichever one she's from—will have a more vested interest in assisting us with our wolf problem, since they'll want her to live in peace and safety."

From a political standpoint, it made sense. An alliance with another kingdom would keep the Vale protected.

But none of that changed the dread I felt at the possibility of marrying someone—being partners with them for an eternity—if I didn't love them.

"Don't look so glum," Laila said. "Think of this as a wonderful opportunity! After all, I could have simply commanded you to wed Camelia, and that would be that. But I care about you, Jacen. I *turned* you. You're like a son to me. Which is why I'm giving you this choice. And the vampire princesses from the other kingdom are some of the strongest, most intelligent, and beautiful women in the entire world. I would think you would be excited for this chance to meet them."

"Meet them?" I raised an eyebrow at her insinuation. "I'm going to be able to leave the Vale?"

"No, no, no." She shook her head. "You won't be going anywhere. After all, *you're* the prince. You're the one they'll be desperate to meet. So they'll be coming to you. All of them at once. We'll make a celebration of it. It'll be the perfect distraction from the growing threat of the wolves. An event like this is exactly what this kingdom needs to boost morale. So, what do you think? The thought of a group of beautiful princesses vying for your heart must hold *some* appeal, does it not?"

"It sounds like a twisted harem." I scowled. "Or a reality television show."

"A show." Her eyes lit up, her mouth opening in excitement. "What a wonderful idea! We'll treat it as a show. Everyone always loves a good show. We'll introduce all of the candidates—the princesses—and interview you all publicly about your dates and thoughts about each other. Perhaps elimination rounds as well? I've seen that done on many of those cheesy television shows that humans love so much." Her eyes went far off, and I could tell her mind was whirling with ideas. "I'll figure it all out," she said. "It'll be such fun."

"Right." I gave her a half smile, my tone dripping with sarcasm. "Sounds like a blast."

"That's hardly the right attitude to have." She pouted. "I'm giving you a wonderful opportunity to find love—like you wanted. You should be thanking me."

"And if I don't fall in love with any of the princesses?" I asked. "What then?"

"I don't advise going into it with that attitude," she

said. "You'll be choosing from the best of the best. Any vampire in the world would *kill* for this opportunity."

"And I would gladly trade spots with them, if they so desired," I said.

"That's not possible." She laughed, her pure joy making me want to cringe. "And remember, if none of the princesses are up to your standards, there's always Camelia. I would happily bless a union with her, if you so desired."

With that, she gave me one final smile, swept herself grandly off my bed, and left the room—leaving me feeling more trapped than ever.

# 10

## ANNIKA

I HURRIED AROUND THE CORNER, following Mike as quickly as possible. We passed by the streets frequented by vampires, then through the drab ones for humans, until finally reaching safety—an alley with barely any lighting. We were nearly invisible in the night, except for the light glow of the moon.

"Score." Mike leaned against the wall, his breathing heavy, and he opened his bag. Inside was a large piece of cheese.

I brightened. Cheese had always been one of my favorite foods, but it was something I rarely got to eat anymore. The piece he'd stolen was a true prize.

It was amazing how much more value the most normal things started to have when they were suddenly scarce or forbidden.

"What'd you get?" he asked me.

"Just a few apples," I replied.

A year ago, apples would have hardly gotten me excited. Now, I imagined the happy faces the others who worked at the Tavern would have when they saw them, and I held my bag closer, as if it contained treasure.

"Want a taste?" Mike broke off a small bit of the cheese and handed it to me.

I took it from him and nibbled at it, wanting to enjoy it as much as possible. It was delicious. Especially compared to the bland food we normally ate.

"Now that we're here—alone—I've been meaning to ask you something." Mike cleared his throat and looked down at me, suddenly serious. With his height, blonde hair, and chiseled jaw, he reminded me of the quarterback of my high school's football team. I imagined he *would* have played high school football—if he hadn't been born and raised in the Vale.

"Okay." I swallowed the final bite of cheese and wrapped my hand around the strap of my bag. "What's up?"

"Christmas is this month," he said.

"It is." I nodded, and my eyes filled with tears. "The first Christmas without my family."

I remembered the last Christmas we'd spent together —how Dad had to run to the store last minute to get the turkey—like he did every year—and how the entire family had come over to celebrate. We'd opened presents under the tree and built gingerbread houses. My brother had refused to follow the instructions, and his came out like a complete mess. We'd joked about how it was a good thing he wanted to be a lawyer and not an engineer. Then he'd knocked my house over—which I'd built perfectly according to the directions—and we'd all eaten until our stomachs were about to burst.

After my time in the Vale, I'd forgotten what being that full felt like.

A tear slipped out, and I wiped it away, standing straighter. I needed to be strong—and I *tried* to be strong. But it was hard.

No one knew about all the nights when I hid under my covers after lights out and allowed the tears to stream quietly from my eyes, as if letting them out could mend my shattered soul.

"I know." Mike reached for my hand and gave it a reassuring squeeze.

I smiled at him and sniffed away the tears, grateful to have him for a friend. More than a friend—as *family*. He could never replace my brother, of course, but I think I would have broken completely if it hadn't been for him.

"Every year on Christmas Eve, there's a celebration

at the village square," he told me. "I was hoping..." He looked down at his feet, his cheeks reddening, and then turned his gaze back up to meet mine. "I was hoping you would go with me. As my date."

I froze, the words sinking in.

A date?

Mike wanted to *date* me?

I had no idea what to think—or to say. Because Mike was awesome. He'd saved my life from that wolf when I first arrived to the Vale, he'd taught me how to get revenge on the vampires by stealing prohibited food, and he'd given me my job at the Tavern.

But I had no romantic feelings for him. And the way he was looking at me right now—with so much hope in his eyes—was breaking my heart.

I didn't want to hurt him. But I needed to be honest with him. Not being honest now, in this moment when he was giving me the chance, would only hurt him more in the long run.

"Well?" he asked, sounding less confident than before. "I know you've been unhappy in the Vale—I understand that. I know you want to leave. When I was younger, I heard tales about the world outside the boundaries, and I used to want to leave too. But *no one* leaves the Vale alive. All we can do is make the best from what we're given. And maybe everything here doesn't have to be horrible. Maybe we can be happy —together."

"Mike," I said his name slowly, wanting to do this as kindly as possible. "I'm flattered. Truly, I am. But we're friends. You've been like family to me since I got here."

He took a deep breath, looking down at me in determination. "I want to see if there can be more between us." He entwined his fingers in mine, as if he didn't want to let me go. "I was hoping you felt the same."

I untangled my hands from his and pulled away. "I don't want to hurt you." I shook my head sadly. "You're my closest friend here. But I don't feel the same way, and I don't want to lead you on. I'm so sorry."

His forehead creased—he looked crushed. I could see the pain shining in his eyes. I wanted so badly to say something—anything—that would make him feel better, but I had no idea what that could possibly be.

Then someone screamed from the street—a blood-curdling shriek that made every hair on my body stand on end.

Mike bolted out of the alley to help, and I was right at his heels.

## 11

## ANNIKA

A WOLF TOWERED in the center of the square, hunched over the body of a young girl as it dug its teeth into her thigh. People ran and screamed, and one lady—who looked the same age as my mom—wailed and tried to force the wolf off the girl.

The wolf snapped its teeth at her and bit a chunk of flesh out of her neck. Blood gushed out of the wound, and the woman held a hand against it, falling to the ground.

I looked around, searching for any vampire guards to take care of the wolf. But this was a human street—so far removed from the vampires that guards didn't bother to come here.

We were on our own. Powerless against a supernatural wolf.

It was yet another reminder of why I hated being so helpless. So *human*.

Most of the humans in the square had run for safety. But Mike reached for a nearby chair and smashed it against his thigh to break off one of the legs. He held it up, and I saw what he'd done—he'd created a weapon. A stake of sorts. It was brilliant.

Following his lead, I grabbed the destroyed chair and broke off another leg to make one for myself. I didn't know what I was doing—I didn't know how to fight. All I knew was how to run and how to climb. But I wasn't leaving Mike here to fight that wolf alone. And if I died in this fight, then at least I'd have died trying to save the village from this monstrous creature.

The wolf was ahead—so involved in its meal that it didn't look at anyone else, and I stared at the weapon in my hand, not knowing what to do with it.

"Get everyone nearby to safety." Mike held the chair leg out in front of him—the pointy end facing out. "I'll deal with the wolf."

I was about to say no—that I wanted to help him fight—but then I noticed a girl standing behind the wolf. Her fingers were in her mouth as she stared at the wolf and cried. She must have been five years old, at the most. She needed to get out of there before the wolf spotted her and decided to make her its next course in its human feast.

I nodded at Mike and ran toward the girl's side, taking her hand in mine. "Come with me," I told her, and I looked around, surveying what was left of the crowd. Most everyone had gotten out of the square by now.

She nodded, and not trusting her to run as fast as I could, I dropped my bag to the ground and pulled her onto my back.

"Hold on," I told her. "Don't let go."

Once she was secured, I darted across the square. I jumped over abandoned delivery carts, landing smoothly and perfectly, not breaking my stride. When we reached the alley, I placed the girl down and glanced over my shoulder to see what was happening with the wolf.

Mike ran toward the wolf, ramming the pointy end into the creature's back.

But it wasn't enough to kill the wolf—it turned around, snarled at Mike, and charged at him.

"Run," I told the girl, taking her hands in mine and pushing her toward the alley. "Run to the Tavern, and tell them Annika sent you."

She turned around and sprinted into the darkness. Once sure she was safe, I hurried back to the square.

The wolf was now facing Mike, and the two of them circled around each other, like predator and prey. They were the only ones who remained in the area—minus the two corpses bleeding out on the ground.

Blood coated the fur around the wolf's mouth, and it licked its lips, as if hungry for more human flesh. Then it bolted forward, and I grabbed the chair leg again, ready to provide backup even though I had no idea what I was doing.

But before I could get halfway there, Mike rammed the wood into the wolf's chest and straight into its heart.

# 12

## ANNIKA

The animal's eyes dimmed, it let out a long breath, and collapsed to the ground.

I stared at the dead animal, to Mike, and then at the two dead women lying in puddles of their own blood. How had this happened? From what I'd learned about the wolves in my year of living here, they had made a pact with the vampires centuries ago. As long as the vampires didn't try to take any more of the wolves land, the wolves would respect the boundaries of the Vale.

The wolves *never* came into the Vale. It was forbidden. After all, us humans "belonged" to the vampires. They needed us for our blood. Wolves were only allowed to attack humans who crossed the boundary.

This wolf coming into the Vale and eating two humans was going to *seriously* piss the vampires off.

Suddenly, someone started clapping from nearby.

At first, the clapping was faint, but it got louder when the person responsible stepped out of a nearby building and under a streetlight.

She was young—I guessed around my age or maybe a few years older—and tall. Her hair was long, dark brown with a hint of red, her features sharp and serious. Her cheeks had a healthy flush—she was human. But her clothes looked fresh and new. Designer jeans, boots, and a leather jacket that probably cost more than humans in the Vale earned in a year.

"Who are you?" I asked, eying her suspiciously.

"Annika." Mike said my name under his breath, reaching for my wrist to stop me from saying anything more. "That's Camelia—advisor to Queen Laila herself."

"But she's human," I pointed out.

"No, dear." The woman—Camelia—smiled. She reminded me of a snake ready to pounce on its prey. "I'm not a human."

"Then what are you?" I asked.

"I'm a witch."

"Oh," I said, and everything clicked into place. I'd always assumed the witch who upheld the boundary was old—around the age of a grandparent. It had never crossed my mind that she could be a few years older than me.

"It's good you're here." Mike stepped forward,

addressing Camelia. "This wolf just came in here and killed these two people. The vampires need to be alerted immediately."

"I'm well aware of what just happened," Camelia said slowly. "I watched the entire thing."

"Oh." Mike's brow creased. "Are the vampires on their way?"

"Not quite." She smiled—as if she had a secret she was about to let us in on. "They will be soon—after all, they'll need to harvest whatever blood is left from the two humans so it doesn't go to waste." She glanced at the corpses in distaste, and my stomach twisted at the realization that of *course* the vampires would milk as much blood from them as possible. "But first, I have a proposition for you."

"For us?" My voice hitched. What could a witch want with two blood slaves? And why had no one else returned to the scene of the crime? I glanced around, realizing for the first time since the attack that the square was still empty.

Now that the wolf was dead, wouldn't other humans want to return and see what had happened?

"I cast a small boundary spell around this square," Camelia said with a wave of her hand, apparently noticing my confusion. "No one will wander here until we've finished our conversation."

"Okay." I stood straighter, unable to hide my curiosity. "What's your proposition?"

She turned to Mike, her eyes hard. "I saw the way you fought off that wolf," she said. "It was impressive—for a human. Therefore, my proposition is for you, and you alone."

"Then why am I here?" I asked.

"As a witness." She barely glanced my way before returning her focus to Mike.

I narrowed my eyes—this was sounding shadier by the second. "If you're able to create a boundary spell to keep people from entering the square, then how did the wolf get into the Vale?" I asked. "Don't you have a bigger version of the spell around the Vale to keep them from entering? Or does it not work with such a big area?"

"You're a witness, not an inquisitor." She rolled her eyes. "Shut up, and let me speak with your friend."

"Answer her question," Mike insisted. "Then I'll hear you out."

"Fine." She huffed, her expression hard. "Yes, I do have a spell over the Vale to keep it hidden and to keep outsiders from entering. The wolves are the only ones who know the location of the Vale. Clearly, they're working with a witch who was able to break through my shield."

"But why would they do that?" I asked. "I thought the vampires and the wolves had a pact?"

"I promised to answer your one question, and I did," Camelia said, and then she turned back to Mike. "Now, for my proposition."

"Yes?" He lifted his chin, waiting for her to continue.

"I have a job I need to fill in the palace."

"What kind of job?" he asked.

"I can't give you the details right now," she said. "But it's a job that can only be completed by a strong, brave, young human like yourself. After watching you defeat that rogue wolf, I know that you're perfect for the task."

"Interesting." He spoke slower than usual, as if considering it. "But what's in it for me?"

"Money," she said simply. "Enough to make sure that you and your family—" She paused to glance at me, and then returned her gaze to Mike. "Will be taken care of for the rest of your lives."

Mike took a deep breath, and I wanted to tell him not to do it. Because whatever this "job" entailed, it must be extremely dangerous for Camelia to offer such a large reward.

"Don't do it," I gave into the urge to tell him, resting a hand on his arm. "You could get hurt. And besides—what could you buy with the money, anyway? Humans are barely allowed anything in the Vale."

Camelia raised a brow. "I'm offering you the deal of

a lifetime," she said. "I can assure you, no human in the history of the Vale has ever received such an offer. Are you truly thinking about turning me down?"

"Not yet," he said, crossing his arms. "But I'd like to negotiate."

She leaned back, shocked. "Very well," she finally said, a small smirk on her face. "What did you have in mind?"

"A lift on the ban of what I can purchase," he said. "Because Annika's right. If I'm going to have all this money, I should be able to spend it on luxuries I can enjoy."

"You'll have to purchase the items in secret," Camelia said. "After all, if the other humans knew that you're being given special privileges, it could cause a riot."

"But I'll be able to buy them?" He leaned forward, gazing at her hungrily. "As long as I keep it secret?"

"Yes." Camelia nodded. "Of course."

"Good." He nodded and leaned back. "How long will I be away?"

"It shouldn't be long." She shrugged. "A week, at the most."

"And how should I explain my absence?"

"The truth," she said. "A top secret job at the palace. And that if you tell anyone the specifics, you—and whoever you tell—will be sent to the dungeons."

I shivered, because even though the humans who were brought to the dungeons were never seen again, we all knew what happened to them. The royal vampires used them as a direct food source until they were drained dry.

Apparently, blood straight from the source was a luxury compared to the blood they took from us each month and refrigerated for the non-royal vampires to consume.

Mike nodded and turned to me. "You'll act as manager at the Tavern until I return," he said, his voice firm. "Inform them of what's going on. Then, once I'm back, we'll never want for anything again."

"You don't have to do this," I begged him, tears filling my eyes at the thought of the danger he could be putting himself in. "We get along fine as we are. You don't have to risk your life like this."

"I'm not just doing it for myself," he said. "I'm doing it for you, for the family I'll have someday, and for everyone else at the Tavern. I'll never get a chance like this again. I want to do this. No—I *have* to do this."

"So you agree to our deal?" Camelia asked.

"I want to learn more about this task you want me to do," he said. "I need to understand *how* dangerous it will be."

"I will tell you." She glanced at me again before returning her gaze to his. "In private. Now, come with me. You'll be returned to the village once your job is complete."

With that, she took him by the arm and whisked him out of the square, not even giving me a chance to say goodbye.

## 13

## CAMELIA

I LED the human boy to my golf cart and drove him out of the village. He didn't say much, instead just staring out the side, his expression solemn. When we came to the road that led to the palace, I turned right, circling away from the imposing building and toward the mountain that loomed over the valley.

"I thought you said the job was in the palace?" he asked.

"I lied," I said simply, staring straight ahead as I drove.

"Why?" he asked.

"Because your girlfriend had already seen enough, and I needed an explanation that she would believe."

His eyes darkened. "She's not my girlfriend."

I smirked—apparently I'd hit a nerve. "Don't look so

glum," I told him. "Once you complete the task I have for you and reap the rewards, I'm sure she'll be throwing herself straight into your arms for a chance to enjoy endless luxuries by your side."

He said nothing, just staring ahead and brooding.

"Don't you want to know more about your task?" I prodded.

"Yes." He didn't look at me when he spoke.

"Good." I smiled. "But first, I want to congratulate you on passing my test."

"Test?" His brow furrowed, and finally he looked at me, confusion swirling in his light blue eyes. "What are you talking about?"

"The wolf." I chuckled. "I let her into the village to see if any humans were strong—and brave—enough to fight her. You were the only one. Congratulations."

Horror dawned on his face. "So you lied about the wolves getting through the boundaries?" he asked. "About them working with a witch? You let innocent people die for a silly *test*?"

"You're getting ahead of yourself." I laughed again. "I didn't lie about the wolves working with a witch and getting through the boundaries. It *did* happen once—remember that old lady found dead in her cabin recently?" He nodded, and I continued. "But of course, I strengthened the boundaries afterward. We're safe for now."

"Stop the cart," he said suddenly. "No more deal. I'm going back."

"No." I pressed harder on the pedal, increasing our speed. "And don't even try to jump out. I've placed a boundary around the cart—you won't be able to leave."

He did exactly as I'd suspected—he ignored me and tried to jump from the cart. Of course, he collided with the invisible shield. He banged his fists against it and grunted, and then turned his angry eyes on me.

"No more deal," he repeated. "Let me out."

"You haven't even learned what I want you to do for me!" I laughed, since I had him now, and he was powerless. "Don't you want all that I've promised you?"

"You're a liar," he said through gritted teeth. "I don't make deals with liars."

"I understand your frustration," I said, since I would doubt myself if I were him as well. But I truly *did* intend on following through with the deal—if he survived the upcoming task. "I lied to you quite a bit—you're right not to trust me."

"So you're going to let me go?" he asked.

"No," I said. "I'd like to make a blood oath."

His mouth dropped open. "Seriously?" he asked.

I couldn't blame him for being surprised. Supernaturals rarely lowered ourselves to making blood oaths with humans. We controlled humans—we didn't bind ourselves to promises with them. But this situation was unique. I needed a human—*this* human—more than he realized.

If it took a blood oath to convince him to trust me, then so be it.

"You'll follow through with our agreement if a blood oath is made?" I asked, parking the cart at the bottom of the mountain.

"Tell me the task first," he said.

"Fine." I sighed. "The task is simple—or at least it's simple for a strong human like you. Do you see the mountain before us? The one with the peak far above the cloud line?"

"Yeah," he said, barely glancing up. "It would be hard to miss it."

"You're to climb up the mountain," I told him. "I've brought all the necessary materials that you'll need—hiking and climbing gear, food and water for the journey, and more. At the top of the mountain, there will be a cave—the Crystal Cavern. Inside the Crystal Cavern is a sapphire ring. I need you to take the ring and bring it to me."

"That's it?" he asked, looking doubtfully up at the mountain.

"That's it," I confirmed.

"Why are you asking me to do this?" he asked, turning to me. "Why not a vampire?"

"Supernatural creatures are forbidden to enter the

Crystal Cavern," I explained. "Only a human can enter —and not just any human. The human must be strong and brave. Which is why I need you."

"Hm." He gazed up at the mountain again, his eyes far off in thought. "What's the catch?" he asked, turning back to me.

"No catch," I said, but then I bit my lip, thinking it through further. "Actually, there is *one* catch."

"Of course there is." He blew out a long breath. "What is it?"

"There will be other objects in the cavern besides the sapphire ring," I told him. "They may look harmless, but I must warn you—those objects are very dangerous. While in the cave, you must only touch the sapphire ring. Do you understand?"

"I understand." He nodded. "And once I bring you this ring, you'll do as you promised?"

"I swear it." I removed a knife from my pocket and ran it over my palm. Blood oozed from the cut, and I stared at the boy daringly, handing the knife to him.

He hesitated—for a moment I feared he wouldn't go through with the deal. But then he took the knife and made an identical cut across his palm.

The moment he did, I took the knife back and grabbed his hand with mine, our open wounds touching. A shock buzzed through my body—the magic of the impending blood oath.

"If you bring me the sapphire ring, I promise to provide you with all the money and luxuries you desire, as long as you tell no one but your family of this deal," I said. "Do you swear to agree to this blood oath?"

"I swear." He kept his gaze locked on mine the entire time. If he were a supernatural, I might have been intimidated.

But he was only human, and thus he had no effect on me.

A light glowed around our hands, the warmth spreading to my body. Then the light dimmed, the blood oath sealed.

"Good." I pulled my hand away from his. As always after blood oaths, both of our cuts had healed. "Now—are you ready to climb that mountain?"

"Yes." He gazed up at the towering peak, looking as determined as he'd appeared before slaughtering that wolf. "I'm ready."

# 14

# CAMELIA

As expected, I waited down at the base of the mountain for days. The boy had a long trek ahead of him, so I'd come prepared.

It was easy to do a warmth spell around my area, and I'd brought a tent, some food, and reading material —a seemingly never ending supernatural series that I'd recently become addicted to. Much of it was incorrect on the abilities of supernaturals, of course, but it was entertaining nonetheless.

While I was technically still within the boundaries of the Vale, it was nice to get away from the drama of the palace for a few days. But finally, on the dusk of the fourth day, I was awoken from sleep by a loud smack next to my tent. I pulled open the zipper and peeked out, my breath catching at the sight before me.

The boy had fallen from the mountain, his body mangled, his skin burned to a crisp. His face had been smashed to a pulp from the fall. The only way I knew it was him was because he was wearing the red hiking shoes I'd provided for his trek.

Then the clouds moved away from the moon, lighting up an object in his hand.

A diamond, glittering in the moonlight.

Well—a *human* would think it was a diamond.

I knew better. I gasped and brought my hands together, shocked at the unexpected present lying at my feet.

Because that wasn't a diamond. It was a seeing crystal. One that had been created by Geneva herself. It had only been rumored of amongst witches, and it was extremely difficult to use, but if handled properly it could apparently answer whatever question a witch asked of it.

Geneva had created the seeing crystal for the use of witches only. If touched by any other creature—supernatural or human—it would kill them instantly. It was a dangerous weapon. That was why the witches had thought it best to lock it away inside the cavern.

The stupid human boy must have been so greedy for wealth that he'd gone against my warning and touched the crystal anyway.

But how close had he been to the sapphire ring? Maybe he'd gotten to the ring *before* the crystal?

I searched his pockets and found nothing. He'd gotten all the way up the mountain, inside the cave, and his stupid greed had been the end of him.

I paced around his corpse, nearly screaming in anger. I'd been so close to getting what I'd wanted.

But I stopped pacing, realization dawning on me. This wasn't the worst thing that could have happened. No... it was a blessing in disguise. Because if—*once*—I learned how to use the seeing crystal, I could ask it exactly how to free Geneva.

I pried the crystal from the dead boy's hand, shoved it inside my bag, and headed back to the palace.

I smiled the entire drive there, knowing I was one step closer to freeing Geneva, marrying Jacen, and finally becoming a vampire.

# 15

# JACEN

THE BLOOD POURED down my throat, and the human went weak in my arms. The warm, delicious liquid called to me, urging me to keep drinking—to drink and drink until I was bursting with it—but if I did that, this human would surely die.

And so, I pulled back.

I took one step away, and then another, wiping the excess blood off my lips. It smeared on my hand, bright and red, and I ran my tongue over it, determined not to let a single drop go to waste.

Then I stared at the twin pinpricks in the woman's neck—at the droplets of blood peeking out from them—but I clenched my fists, digging my nails into my palms and forcing myself to back away until I stood against the opposing wall.

The woman opened her eyes, looking wearily around the room.

"Take her away," I ordered to Laila.

"Are you sure?" the vampire queen asked. "She's still alive. There's more blood left..." She took a deep breath, indulging in the exquisite aroma. "It smells *so* delicious."

"Take her away!" I glared at the human, aware of each pump of her heart as it sent blood rushing through her veins. But I forced myself to take shallow breaths. The shallower my breathing, the less sensitive I would be to the tantalizing scent that urged me to keep drinking until the woman was drained dry.

"Only if you're sure." Laila's voice was silky and smooth—I might have even thought she sounded seductive, if she wasn't annoying me to death.

I huffed and turned to Daniel. "Take her away," I said steadily, looking straight into his eyes and putting as much power into my voice as possible.

Compelling him.

His face went slack, and he picked up the human, carrying her out of the room.

Once the doors closed behind them, I allowed myself to breathe normally again. I looked at Laila, waiting for her to say something. We were the only two in the room now—Camelia had been noticeably distant since my refusal of her proposal earlier this month.

At least she seemed to be accepting my rejection with dignity.

"I see you've been improving your compulsion," Laila observed.

"I have," I said.

"And that's seven days in a row that you've been able to stop yourself while feeding."

"It is." I nodded. "I'm able to control myself around humans now."

"In a sanctioned setting," she pointed out.

I waited for her to continue—waited for her to say that it was time to move onto something bigger. That I was ready to leave the palace.

She said nothing.

"I'm ready to leave the palace now," I said, since clearly she wasn't going to say it first. "This past week has proven that."

"Perhaps." Laila smirked and raised an eyebrow.

"What else do you need me to do to prove myself?" I asked, raising my voice at her again. I knew she was a queen and that she technically deserved respect, but she frustrated me to hell, so screw the rules. "Do you need to bring a whole *crew* of humans in here to tempt me? If so, then do it! Do whatever's necessary for you to trust me."

"When you're ready, I'll know," she said, giving me that irritatingly knowing smile of hers. "In the meantime, it's Christmas Eve. I have some tasks to attend to in order to get the palace ready for tomorrow. I'll see you soon."

She smiled at me one more time, swished her dress around herself, and left the room.

# 16

# JACEN

I'D BEEN PACING around my room for the past hour since Laila had left, deep in thought. What more did she expect of me? How many more humans did I have to successfully feed from before she trusted me enough to leave the palace? It almost seemed like she *enjoyed* keeping me here.

Like she was purposefully keeping me prisoner.

Music and voices started to fill the village—Christmas Eve and Christmas Day were apparently two of the few days each year that the humans were allowed to let loose and celebrate.

Excited chatter drifted through my window, and I couldn't help thinking about my last Christmas—how I'd insisted on going to swimming practice instead of spending the entire day with my family. I'd always been so goal-oriented and ambitious, putting my Olympic medal dreams before everything else. I'd refused to slack off, not even for a holiday. After all, I wouldn't be in my athletic prime forever. I'd figured I would have more time with my family *after* I'd completed my goals.

I'd never expected that my life would be taken from me in a single night. That I would never see my family again.

They thought I was dead.

It was probably better for them to think that. They would never accept me for what I was now—a monster.

Hell, *I* didn't even accept myself as I was now.

Even if I got a chance to see them again, I had no place in the human world anymore. It was best for all of us if they continued believing I was dead.

But I missed being human. I missed being around people who were relaxed and happy—people who treated me as an equal. People who I could just have *fun* with.

I hadn't had any fun since... well, I supposed I hadn't had any fun since before becoming a vampire. The other vampires looked at me as some kind of project. The poor, vampire prince who was turned against his will and couldn't gain control over his bloodlust. They were either jealous of me for being vampire royalty, pitied me for it, or they hated me for it. Nothing in between. And they refused to get close to me, since most of them figured I would eventually lose my mind to the bloodlust and off myself.

How was I expected to *live* like this?

I stopped pacing and stared out the window. The streets were lit up more than I'd ever seen them before. The music got louder, and I heard laughter and chatter —the sounds of people having fun.

I wanted to be there. With them. Not as a vampire prince—but as me. As Jacen.

Maybe I *could* go out there.

I could now be around humans and control my bloodlust. After this past week, I knew I could stop myself from feeding once I'd started. And I'd been practicing my compulsion. Compelling vampires was harder than compelling humans, but I seemed to have gotten the hang of it.

Since I had all these powers, I might as well put them to good use and attempt to sneak out of the palace. After all, there were only a few ways this could end.

I could fail at compelling multiple guards and end up exactly where I was now—stuck inside the palace.

I could escape, not be able to handle myself around so many humans, and go on another murder spree. If that happened, I hoped Laila would do what she should have done the first time I'd gone on a rampage—put me out of my misery forever. If she didn't, perhaps that would be the breaking point I needed to do it myself.

Or I could escape, kill no one, and prove once and for all that I was capable of being free to roam the Vale as I pleased.

I was neutral about the first option.

I refused to let the second happen.

The third was what I wanted.

Since becoming a vampire, I'd lost who I'd been as a human. It hurt too much to think about the life I had before—the life I would never get back. But now, I forced myself to remember. Because my swimming coach had always told me—goal setting was about mindset. If you saw yourself completing your goal and believed you could do it, you would reach it. Train. Push yourself. *Make* your goals happen.

That was exactly what I planned on doing tonight.

# 17

## ANNIKA

I STARED out the window of the attic crawl space, watching as people walked excitedly along the streets. It was my first Christmas in the Vale, and it was by far the happiest I'd ever seen the humans in the village.

They strolled casually down the streets, chatting, laughing, and drinking. Alcohol was one of the few indulgences us humans in the Vale were allowed—low-end alcohol, but we weren't picky—although I rarely chose to drink. I'd always found that drinking escalated my emotions. And since I'd been mostly sad since coming to the Vale, drinking made it worse. So I stayed away from alcohol.

Even though everyone seemed so excited, I couldn't imagine going out and having fun tonight. So I was set on remaining here—in the cozy attic crawl space.

The crawl space wasn't huge, but I'd made it my own. With the bookshelves and few blankets that I'd brought up here, it was my own little reading nook. No one else liked to come here—I supposed they felt cramped—but I loved it. It was the only place I could get away and lose myself in books without being disturbed.

The back window also had an incredible view of the palace.

I didn't know what went on inside of the palace—probably horrible things. But the building itself was so huge and impressive, built into the side of the mountain, that despite the horrors that happened inside, looking at it gave me hope that all the beauty in my world wasn't lost forever. And once Mike returned—whenever that would be—I hoped that the stories he had to recount from his time in the palace wouldn't *all* be bad.

For now, I picked up the book I was reading, opened it to the bookmarked page, and settled in to enjoy the story.

It wasn't long before someone started banging on the entrance in the floor.

"Annika!" someone yelled—Tanya, one of the other girls who worked at the Tavern. She'd been brought to the Vale around the same time I was, and besides Mike, she was my closest friend here. "Are you up there?"

I said nothing, not wanting to be disturbed.

She opened the entrance to the crawl space and peeked inside anyway. "I thought I would find you here," she said, opening the trap door fully and pushing herself up. "You aren't *seriously* going to stay up here for all of Christmas, are you?"

"Umm..." I glanced down at the book in my lap, since yes, that was exactly what I'd planned to do.

"No." Tanya widened her big brown eyes and shook her head. "You are absolutely not staying in this dingy attic and reading a book on Christmas Eve."

"Why not?" I asked, pulling the book closer. "It's not like I have anything to celebrate anymore."

She climbed up into the crawlspace with me, shutting the door under her. "That's not true," she said, her eyes serious now. "I know that *this* isn't the life you imagined for yourself, but you're still alive. You have me. And Mike. Friends till the end, right?"

"I might be alive, but I don't get to *live*," I told her. "There's a difference."

"Don't be like that." She pouted. "We all lost everything when we were brought here. It sucks. Trust me, I know."

I nodded, since I *did* know. Tanya had been on a school trip when she'd been abducted. She, her boyfriend, her friend Maria, and Maria's boyfriend had snuck out after curfew. She and Maria had watched their boyfriends be murdered in front of them—sucked dry by the vampires. The two of them were then brought here.

Maria hadn't lasted a month in the Vale before taking her own life.

"Everyone says that Christmas Eve and Christmas Day are the best days for humans in the Vale," Tanya continued. "It's one of the few days the vampires don't force us to work. Don't you at least want to *try* going out and having fun? At least for me? You're the closest friend I have here—the party won't be any fun without you."

I didn't, actually. But I could tell by the way Tanya was looking at me—her eyes wide and hopeful—that she was only going to be able to have fun tonight if I at *least* gave it a chance and went with her.

"Fine." I sighed and marked my spot in the book, putting it back on the shelf. "But only because you forced me."

18

# ANNIKA

I SHOWERED, put on the nicer of the two pairs of jeans I owned, and allowed Tanya to style my hair. I'd never been a fan of my hair—it was brown, long, and thin. Boring. The only thing good about it was that it was easy to take care of.

Tanya did some fancy medieval braided hairstyle for me and brought me over to the mirror to see. Of course, I had no makeup on—humans in the Vale had no access to makeup—but with my hair all clean and done up, it was the prettiest I'd felt since I'd arrived.

It was the first time I felt like a *human* and not like a slave.

"Thank you." I turned to Tanya, my eyes filling with tears, and gave her a hug. "Really."

"Anytime." She did a final adjustment to my hair,

bringing the loose parts over my shoulders. "Now, are you ready to party or what?"

"I'm ready." I smiled, surprised that it wasn't a total lie, and followed her out the door.

---

I'd never seen the streets in the village so *alive*. People drank, chatted, and even danced in the main square. A tree had been placed in the center. People had wound what looked like rolled up bed sheets around it, and used common kitchen items as ornaments. Mainly forks, knives, and spoons, but there were a few decorated cups thrown into the mix as well.

It wasn't much, but at least they'd worked with what we had to create *some* feeling of festivity.

Tanya and I found the rest of the group from the Tavern, and the moment they saw us, they pulled us into their circle and complimented me on my hair.

"It's all Tanya's doing," I said with a shrug. "I just sat there and let her work her magic."

"Well, it looks great," one of the guys—Kyle—said, handing each of us a beer.

I refused and opted for a soda instead.

"By the way, we were just talking about Mike," Kyle added after I'd taken my first sip.

"What about him?" I asked, instantly going on guard.

Because while I didn't want anyone to know, I was worried about Mike. Camelia had said the job he needed to do would only take a few days.

It had been over two weeks, and there was still no word from him.

She would have let me know if something had happened to him… right?

"Shouldn't he be back by now?" Kyle asked.

"I don't know," I said, since Camelia had never told me the exact day he would be returned. "I guess his job in the palace is taking longer than they anticipated."

"I wish *I'd* been chosen for a job in the palace," Tanya said dreamily, gazing up at the majestic building on the mountain. "I wonder if he'll be allowed to tell us what it's like there?"

"Even if he isn't, we need to *force* him to tell us," one of the other girls—Valerie—chimed in.

I nodded in agreement, although I couldn't push the worry away.

Hopefully Mike would be back soon.

"What do you all know about Camelia?" I asked, wanting to change the subject. "The witch who works for Queen Laila."

"Nothing," Kyle said. "Except that she upholds the boundary around the Vale."

"And that she's the reason why the temperatures

here are bearable," Valerie added. "We would probably all freeze to death if it wasn't for her magic."

"Anything else?" I asked. "Do you think she's honest?"

As in—would she lie about what she truly needed Mike to do? Because what if she didn't need him for a job in the palace at all? What if she took him for something else?

What if he was never coming back?

"I don't know." Kyle shrugged. "It's not like she's ever talked to any of us."

"Yeah." Valerie finished off her beer and started a new one. "Not even those of us who grew up here!"

I sighed and gazed up at the mountain. The palace was so close, yet so far away.

What were the vampires doing in there right now? I imagined their Christmas celebration was incredible and decadent.

"Don't look so glum," Tanya said to me. "I'm sure he's fine."

"Thanks." I forced a smile, although I could tell she knew that it wasn't real.

"I love this song!" She grabbed my hand, pulling me to the center of the square. "Come on—let's dance!"

I allowed her to drag me away, because I didn't feel like standing there and discussing Mike for any longer. The others followed, and soon enough we were all dancing in the square, singing along and cheering each other on. It reminded me of what my life had been like *before*.

And while I knew it wouldn't last for long, I was determined to enjoy it.

# 19

## JACEN

I STEPPED through the door in the palace walls, thinking about how easy it had been to compel the vampire guards to let me pass. All I'd had to do was look at them, command them to let me by, and that was it.

They'd moved to the side and allowed me to go on my way.

The palace was abuzz with preparations to celebrate Christmas Eve at midnight, so it was relatively empty outside. Using my vampire speed, I zipped down the mountain, feeling *alive* as the wind knocked off my hood and rushed through my hair. This wasn't the first time I'd been outside the palace—I would never forget the first time and the massacre that had followed—but this was the first time when I wasn't overcome by the haze of bloodlust.

Last time, the scent of blood coming from the humans in the village had consumed me.

Now, while I smelled their blood, and while I *wanted* it, I controlled it. And instead of only thinking about the blood, I thought about other things. Like how the mountains towered so high that this valley truly felt like a kingdom, and how the air was so crisp and clean that it took my breath away.

I took the back roads, not wanting to run into any vampires (even though I now fully trusted my ability to compel them), and finally arrived at the human village.

It was easy to tell where the vampire town ended and the human village began, and not just because the smell of their blood became infinitely stronger with each step I took. In the village, the houses were shabbier, the cobblestones on the streets were uneven and unturned, and everything in general was much more drab.

I pulled on my hood and stopped in the path, looking around. Why had I wanted to come here at all? Being here—seeing the way the human blood slaves lived—it was depressing.

But then a song started playing in the distance—a popular song I remembered from before being brought to the Vale. People hooted and hollered—it sounded like they were having *fun*.

I wanted to join them.

I wanted to stop being Prince Jacen, the newly turned vampire who couldn't control his bloodlust, and become another face in the crowd.

And so, I hurried toward the music, making sure to keep a normal pace. After all, no one would believe I was a human if I burst in there running at the speed of a vampire.

As I got closer, the streets got busier. People were holding bottles of what looked like home brewed beer, and they were all headed in the same direction I was—toward the sound of music.

Then one of them bumped up against me, his neck tantalizingly close to my lips.

I imagined what it would be like to pull him into a dark corner, dig my fangs into his neck, and drink his blood dry. But he smelled like something else—alcohol—and that alone made it easier to stop my fangs from sliding out of my gums. Alcohol gave blood a bitter aftertaste—it was why when humans donated their blood once a month, they were required to refrain from drinking alcohol for twenty-four hours beforehand.

I'd once asked Laila why humans were allowed alcohol at all. Weren't they considered slaves and forbidden from all luxuries?

She'd told me that when you ruled, it was important

to not take *everything* away from your subjects. It was necessary to give them a bit of what they desired—alcohol, a few days off a year, books, etc. Those small allowances gave them hope.

Hope lowered the chance of rebellion.

But only a bit of it. Too much, and then there might be trouble.

Now that I'd gained control over my bloodlust, I glared at the guy who'd bumped into me and walked away.

"Sorry," he muttered under his breath. Once he thought I was out of his hearing, he told his friend, "What'd I ever do to him?"

I didn't pay attention to the friend's answer. I just walked faster, toward the music, feeling more confident now that I knew the humans were drinking tonight.

The alcohol in their systems would make it *much* less likely that I would lose control.

Finally, I approached a square—I guessed it was the main square in the village, because it was packed with people celebrating and dancing.

In the center was the saddest Christmas tree I'd ever seen. The tree itself was average, but the decorations were pathetic. What looked like twisted bed sheets were wound around it, and instead of ornaments there was kitchenware. Actual *kitchenware* that people ate with—forks, spoons, knives, and the like.

I looked around in bewilderment. All of this partying for this sad little Christmas tree?

But as I took in the happy faces, I realized how condescending I was being. The humans here didn't have access to traditional Christmas decorations. The fact that they had come together, taken their everyday objects, and made use of them where they could was... well, I daresay it was *magical.*

A few people looked my way, and I pulled my hood farther over my head, trying to shrink into the wall. I imagined I looked quite silly—at over six feet tall, with the physique of an Olympian swimmer, I'd never been one to hide in the shadows.

But I couldn't afford having anyone recognize me. I doubted they would—I hadn't yet been introduced as a prince of the Vale since I technically hadn't proven control over my bloodlust, and they *certainly* would never think that a vampire would come to their Christmas Eve celebration—but it was better to be safe than sorry.

I was looking around, watching everyone chat and laugh and dance, when I saw her.

She was dancing with her friends, but the first thing I noticed was her hair. The color wasn't anything special—brunette, like many others in the crowd—but she wore it in an intricate half braided style. When she smiled, she looked like a princess. Her cheeks were flushed and radiant—I assumed from dancing—and her eyes were warm and kind as she chatted with a small blonde girl next to her.

I wanted her to look at *me* like that. With such pure happiness and kindness.

I wanted to know her.

And so, I pushed through the crowd, unaware of anything but the beautiful girl before me. I wasn't even aware of the smell of their blood.

Finally I neared her group, and I stood there watching them, unsure what to say.

Why was I so speechless? In my human life, I'd approached so many beautiful women at bars that I'd lost count. I had this down to an art.

But that was my human self.

Now I was a vampire.

That was what had made me pause. Because this girl —whoever she was—looked so kind and innocent. I wanted her, yes. But did I want to taint her with who I was? I could already smell her blood above everyone else's—sweet, delicious, and untainted by alcohol. Why didn't she drink when all the other humans reveled in such a luxury?

The question only made me want to know her more —to discover the answer.

But if I did… and if I was alone with her… who knew what I would do? I could already envision myself sinking my fangs into her neck—enjoying the rush as her blood poured down my throat and filled my body.

I forced the thought from my mind. I couldn't let myself think like that. I'd gained control over my bloodlust in the past week—I'd proven it many times.

But what if I lost control again?

What if this innocent girl died because of me?

"Hello?" someone spoke to me—the short blonde standing next to the girl—jarring me from my thoughts. "Do you want something?"

The four of them in the circle stopped dancing and looked at me. My eyes went straight to the brunette's. She, too, watched me with curiosity. But her eyes were no longer open and sweet. They were guarded and full of questions. Her posture had stiffened, and she stood strong, as if ready to defend herself.

Still, she was beautiful. Regal. Fascinating.

And in just that moment—as if the universe were acting in my favor—a slow song started to play.

"Would you like to dance?" I asked, my gaze locked on hers.

Her friends all looked at her, and the blonde girl even smirked.

I was barely able to breathe as I waited for her response. How had this one girl—this human—bewitched me so quickly?

"Annika?" the blonde said, squeezing the brunette's

arm. “Aren’t you going to say yes?”

“Annika,” I repeated, her name rolling easily off my tongue. “One dance. That’s all I ask.”

I held out a hand, and her friends backed away, leaving only the two of us standing there.

The girl—Annika—still looked at me with suspicion, and I had a feeling that gaining her trust was going to be a challenge. But it was a challenge I wanted to take. After all, I was strong. I could resist the call of her blood.

So I made a promise to myself—a promise that I would never hurt her. And I knew, deep in my soul, that it was a promise I would keep.

“Fine,” she finally said, her gaze not leaving mine. “On one condition.”

“And what’s that?” I was taken aback that she hadn’t accepted instantly—in my human life, most girls I’d approached were always interested—but I didn’t let my surprise show.

“You tell me your name.”

“Ja—,” I started, but then I realized I couldn’t say my real name. The humans in the village might not know what I looked like, but they’d *certainly* heard the name of the latest addition to the vampire royal family. “Jake,” I said, catching myself before I’d finished saying my name.

"Okay, Jake." She nodded and placed her hand in mine, her eyes glinting with challenge. "Let's dance."

# 20

# ANNIKA

I DIDN'T KNOW what had prompted me to say yes to this man.

At first I'd assumed he wanted what most guys wanted at a celebration like this—to see how far they could get with me. But those guys—the "players," as my friends and I had called them back home—almost always tended to be drunk. And despite the hood creating shadows over his face, I knew that Jake wasn't drunk. Because his eyes—such a unique shade of gray that they could almost be described as silver—were focused and clear.

He looked somewhat familiar, but I would never forget eyes like those, especially the contrast they had with his dark hair. And he was watching me so intensely that it felt like he was gazing straight into my soul.

When I said yes, I was as surprised as anyone. But I'd already said it, so there was no taking it back.

He reached his hand out to take mine, and his skin was so cold that I nearly flinched.

"What?" He stepped closer, placing his other arm around my back and pulling me toward him.

"Nothing," I said. "It's just—your hand is so cold."

Something crossed over his eyes—panic, perhaps? But then they were cool and confident again. "Maybe you're just warm," he said with a smirk.

"Maybe." I rolled my eyes, because if that was some kind of pick up line, it was pretty lame.

We swayed in time to the music, and I found myself at a loss for words. It had been so long since I'd attended a party like this. I supposed I was out of practice.

"I don't think I've seen you around before," he finally broke the silence. "Have you lived here your whole life?"

"No," I said sadly, holding onto him tighter. "I was brought here a little less than a year ago."

"So it's your first Christmas in the Vale," he realized.

I nodded in response, not trusting my voice to stay steady if I spoke.

"It's mine too," he said.

"When were you taken?" I asked, glad to have found this common ground between the two of us.

"A little less than a year ago," he said. "Just like you."

"A lot of us were taken around then," I said.

"They were." His eyes darkened—he must not like remembering his story of how he was brought here any more than I liked remembering mine. I couldn't blame him… but I was also curious about his story.

Then I realized why he looked so familiar.

"I recognize you," I said slowly. "Or at least I think I do."

"Really?" He raised an eyebrow. "Because I know we haven't met before. You're not someone I could ever forget."

My cheeks flushed, and I cursed my body for betraying his effect on me. "You remind me of that swimmer," I said. "The one who was on track for the Olympics."

"You follow sports?" he asked.

"I was a gymnast." I shrugged. "I was never good enough to try for the Olympics, but I was hoping to compete in college."

"But now you're here." His deadpan tone got across what he meant—that now I would never be able to compete in the sport that I'd previously dedicated my life to.

"Yes," I said. "Now I'm here."

I waited for him to answer my question—to tell me if he was that swimmer—but he said nothing. I supposed I would have to prod further.

"Am I right?" I asked. "About who you are? Well... who you were? Before being brought here?"

"No." He laughed. "I do get that a lot though. Apparently I look a lot like him."

"You do," I agreed, hoping I hadn't made him feel insignificant by comparing him to a minor celebrity. "And that's a good thing. I always thought he was attractive. So I meant it as a compliment." I shut my mouth immediately afterward, realizing that I sounded like a babbling idiot.

His eyes shined in amusement. "If you meant it as a compliment, then I'll take it as one," he said.

We continued to dance, and I sunk into his arms, inwardly thanking Tanya for forcing me to come out tonight.

Then the music went off—before the song ended. It was like someone had pulled the plug.

People groaned and complained in the crowd.

"What's going on?" I pulled away from Jake and looked for my friends. My heart rose in my throat when I couldn't find them where I'd left them.

"Vampires." Jake whispered in my ear. "Look."

I looked at where he was facing, and sure enough,

five vampires dressed in their black guard uniforms stood around the Christmas tree.

What were they doing here? Vampires never guarded the human village. The wolves were enough of a threat to keep us out of trouble. We were usually guarded by higher up humans— usually the humans who had generations of family in the Vale. Vampires were only called in for emergencies.

Judging by the hushed chatter throughout the crowd, I wasn't the only one who was confused.

"I need to leave," Jake said, his eyes darting around the square. "Now."

"Why?" I held tighter onto his hand, not ready to let him go. I had no idea if I would see him again.

And if he was in trouble... I wanted to help. Which was silly, because I barely knew him, but I wanted to help nonetheless.

"They're looking for me." He pulled the hood higher over his head and turned away from the guards.

"Why?" I asked.

Because what would they want with a human from the Vale?

There was only one answer I could think of—they wanted to bring him into the dungeons of the palace.

If he was brought there... he would never come back.

"Never mind why," I said, not giving him a chance to

answer—and still not letting go of his hand. The guards all blocked the road that led to the vampire's town, but the street leading to the Tavern was unmanned. "I know a place where you can hide."

"Where is this place?" he asked, his voice low.

"Somewhere secret," I told him. "They won't find you, I promise."

"You trust me?" He raised an eyebrow, and I was surprised to find a hint of playfulness in his silver eyes. "Even though we just met?"

"I'm not sure why, but yes," I said, not needing to stop to think about my answer. "And if we want a shot at getting away, we have to go now."

He gave me a small nod, and I led him out of the crowd, breaking into a run the moment we turned into the nearest alley.

## 21

# JACEN

I KEPT UP WITH ANNIKA, impressed by her speed. However, it held nothing on mine, and I had to focus on running slowly as to not give away the fact that I wasn't human.

As we ran, I questioned my decision to go with her. It hadn't been an easy decision to make. Because if the vampire guards had found me, they might have revealed who I was.

*What* I was.

Once Annika knew I wasn't human, she would never look at me the same again. And the way she'd looked at me while we'd been dancing—with interest, and perhaps even intrigue—I didn't want to lose that. At least not yet.

So I went with her.

She navigated the alleyways so fluidly—like a choreographed dance. I supposed it was the gymnast in her. Finally, we rounded a corner, and she stopped at a wooden building with a sign above the door that said The Tavern.

"This is your secret place?" I asked. "A bar?"

"Above the bar." She looked up at the highest window. "But if anyone sees us come in the front door, they'll ask about you. So… how good are you at climbing?"

"Up there?" I glanced worriedly at the window. Not because I thought I couldn't do it—as a vampire, climbing the wall would be easy—but because I was worried about her.

"Yes." She nodded.

"Have you ever done this before?" I asked.

"A few times." She shrugged. "It's pretty easy to climb, as long as you know the right places to hold onto."

"You first," I told her—because while she seemed confident, I wanted to be there to catch her if she fell. "I'll follow your lead."

"All right." She smiled and bounded toward the side of the building, placing her hands and feet in each spot with ease as she made her way up the side. She looked like Rapunzel climbing up her tower.

I held my breath, sure she was about to make a

wrong move. But she made it up so gracefully that if she'd said she was a vampire, I would have believed her.

Once at the top, she opened the window and hoisted herself inside. "Come on," she called out, her hair blowing in the wind. "I'll guide you if you get stuck."

"I won't get stuck." I smirked, ready for the challenge, and rushed toward the building. My abilities would have easily allowed myself to jump from the ground to the window, but I went at the same pace she'd climbed. Anything else would have been a dead giveaway that I wasn't who I'd claimed to be.

"Wow," she said as I made my way inside the cramped attic. "That was impressive."

"I told you it wouldn't be a problem." I looked out the window as she closed it, making sure the vampire guards hadn't followed us.

The streets were clear.

Confident that we'd gotten away, I relaxed and looked around the room. When I'd first seen the lone window on the top of the building, I'd assumed it was going to be a dusty old attic. And while it *was* an attic—the low ceilings nearly brushed the top of my head—it had been transformed into a cozy book nook. There was a shelf packed with books—both new and old—and blankets strewn about to create a spot for reading.

"Where does that look out to?" I glanced at the

window on the opposite side, which was blocked by curtains.

Annika smiled—so big that it reached her eyes. "Come," she said, making her way to the other end of the room. "I'll show you."

She opened the curtains, revealing an incredible view of the palace on the mountain.

My prison.

"It's beautiful." Her eyes shined as she gazed up at it. "Don't you think?"

"It's full of vampires," I said sharply.

"You hate them," she observed, turning to look at me.

"Yes." I didn't need to think about my answer. I hated vampires—and I hated that I was one of them. "Don't you?"

"I hate that they killed my family," she said, sounding stronger than ever. "I hate that they're keeping me prisoner here. But more than I hate them, I hate being weak. I hate being human."

"What?" I knew I must be looking at her like she was crazy, but I didn't care. Because what she'd said *was* crazy. "If you hate being human, what would you rather be?"

"A vampire," she said simply.

"No." I shook my head and backed away, flashes of the faces of all the people I'd killed rushing through my mind. "The vampires are killers. *Murderers*. Why would you want to be like them?"

*Like me,* I thought, although of course I didn't say it out loud.

"First of all, most of them can control their urges," she said, as if she'd done full research on the topic. "They drink the blood we donate instead of killing humans."

"Controlling those urges isn't as easy as you make it sound," I muttered.

"Really?" She tilted her head, watching me closely. "How would you know?"

I wracked my mind for an explanation that *wouldn't* give away my secret. "Don't you know about that vampire who got loose last year and killed all those villagers?" I asked. "I *know* you must know—everyone knows. It's why they needed to go on all those scouting missions to bring back new humans for the village. It's why they took you."

"And you," she said, reminding me of the story I'd told her earlier when we were dancing.

"Why would you want to become a creature like that?" I asked.

"Most of them aren't like that." She straightened, looking fully convinced. "That vampire who rampaged the village was killed by order of the queen."

"Really?" I couldn't help but chuckle. If only she knew...

"Yes," she said. "But that's not the point."

"Then tell me," I asked. "What *is* your point?"

She glanced back up at the palace, took a deep breath, and turned back to me. "As humans, we'll always be weak compared to the supernaturals," she said, clenching her fists by her sides. "We have no chance against them. We'll always be slaves to the vampires. But if I were one of them, I would be free." Her eyes were so full of fire and determination—I knew she believed it.

And on a certain level, she was right. The vampires would never let her leave the Vale. She would be a blood slave until she died.

She also had no chance of becoming a vampire, since each person turned in North America had to be approved by Laila. Any vampires turned without her approval were killed.

Human blood slaves were considered the lowest of the low. They were farm animals—a food source.

Laila never had, and never would, consider one of them worthy of becoming a vampire. Which was a good thing, because I hated the thought of Annika risking her life to become a monster.

"What?" she asked, tilting her head in curiosity. "Are

you realizing that I'm right? That becoming a vampire is the only way for us to ever be truly free?"

"It's irrelevant," I said. "They would never turn you. Or any of us, for that matter."

"I know," she said, and then she turned back to gaze at the palace. "But it doesn't hurt to dream."

Looking at her now—at this seemingly delicate human girl who had somehow managed to stay strong despite what she'd been through at the hands of the vampires—I realized that there was nothing more I wanted than to step closer to her, look into her eyes again, and kiss her.

If I'd been human—if I were Jake and not Jacen, and if the story I'd told her had been true—I would have done exactly that.

But it *did* hurt to dream. Because I would never be human. And if I kissed her, I feared I might lose control and crave a taste of her blood. I would stop myself from draining her—I trusted my control enough to risk coming out here tonight—but then she would know that everything I'd told her so far had been a lie.

No matter how much I admired her strength, resilience, and hope, and no matter how much I wanted to get to know her better, the two of us had no future. By being here with her, I was living in a fantasyland as much as she was every time she gazed up at the palace and dreamed of becoming a vampire.

Maybe in another life we would have worked out. But not in this one.

There was only one honorable thing I could do at this point—compel her to forget me. I hated the thought of it, but it would be best for both of us. Because coming here with her—trusting her and starting to build a connection with her—was a mistake.

"Annika," I said her name slowly, savoring each syllable as I spoke it.

"What?" She turned to me, her eyes full of hope.

She was looking at me the way I'd hoped she would when I'd first spotted her in the square, and the trust in her eyes took my breath away.

"You're going to forget you ever met me," I said calmly, feeling the magic of compulsion in my voice as I spoke. "Tonight, you were dancing with your friends when the vampire guards showed up. You got scared and ran back here—alone—and fell asleep reading." I reached for a book sitting on top of the shelves—a bookmark stuck out from it, so I assumed it was the one she was currently reading—and handed it to her.

She didn't take it.

"What?" She backed away, her forehead creased with hurt, her fists clenched by her sides. "Why do you want me to pretend we never met?"

## 22

## ANNIKA

"It's for the best," Jake said, his intense gaze not leaving mine. "You're going to erase me from your memory completely."

I took the book and tossed it onto the blankets. "I don't understand," I said, wanting—no, *needing*—to get to the bottom of this. "Is this connected to why you ran away from the vampire guards?"

"Yes." The intensity left his gaze, and it turned into something else. Confusion.

I thought back on the entire night—dancing with him, the guards showing up, and bringing him here. I waited for him to continue, but he didn't. He just stood there, watching me.

Something wasn't adding up. And there was no way

I was going to forget we ever met. I couldn't forget him, not even if I wanted to.

"I put myself at risk bringing you here tonight." I crossed my arms, irritated now. "The least you can do is give me some answers."

"I can't." His eyes darted around the attic, as if searching for a way out. "I have to go."

"Where are you going?" I asked.

"Home," he replied. "And if you're thinking about trying to follow me—don't."

I took a step back, rejection and hurt swirling through my chest. I didn't get it. As silly as it sounded, I'd felt a connection with Jake while we were dancing. I wouldn't have taken him here if I hadn't. I'd thought he felt it, too. After all, he was the one who'd asked me to dance. He was the one who'd agreed to come with me, and who seemed to be enjoying spending time with me. Now he wanted me to forget him?

What could he possibly be involved with that would make him scared of the vampires?

Unless we broke one of their rules, the vampires protected the humans in the village. They needed to, since we were their food.

The only reason to be scared of them was if you'd broken one of their laws and feared being taken to the dungeon.

"Are they trying to arrest you?" I asked. "Is that why you needed to run?"

"No," he said curtly.

"Then why did you need to hide from them?"

"I can't tell you that." He looked away from me, his expression hard.

"I'll keep your secret." I stepped closer and took his hand in mine, hoping it would convince him to open up to me and stay. "I promise."

He hesitated, and for a moment I thought I'd convinced him—that he was going to tell me what he was hiding.

"I can't." He pulled his hand out of mine, and my heart fell at his rejection. "But I do have a question for you."

"Okay." I straightened, hoping that this question would get me closer to figuring out some answers.

"Do you—or the others at the Tavern—have access to wormwood?" he asked.

"No," I said instantly. "We're not allowed to have wormwood. You know that. If it's in our system, our blood tastes bad to the vampires."

"I wasn't asking if you ingested wormwood," he said. "I was asking if you have access to it. Or if you're wearing it right now."

"No," I repeated, and I took a step back, unsure what was going on. We truly didn't have any wormwood here—if we were found with it, it was grounds for being taken to the dungeons.

Was he working undercover for the vampires? Did they suspect that the Tavern was growing wormwood and were sending him to investigate?

I didn't know why they would do that instead of simply storming the Tavern themselves.

Unless he was trying to get wormwood himself? Maybe he was trying to rebel against the vampires?

Maybe he wanted to attempt escape?

"Why are you asking?" I spoke slowly and softly, hoping it would help him open up to me. "Whatever it is, you can trust me. I won't tell anyone. I promise."

"I know I can trust you," he said.

"Then tell me what's going on," I begged. "So I can help you."

"You've already done more than enough," he said. "My problems are my own, and I can handle them from here."

"So you're leaving?" I asked. "Just like that?"

"I have to."

Clearly I wasn't going to get any more information out of him tonight. But at the same time, for reasons I didn't understand, I couldn't bear the thought of never seeing him again. If we never saw each other again, I would fear the worst—that he'd been imprisoned, or that he'd tried to escape and had been killed by the wolves. I would always blame myself for not trying harder to help him right now.

"I know you asked me to forget you, but I can't do that," I said, forcing myself to stay strong. "So before you go, can you answer one more question?"

"Depends on what that question is." He smirked.

It took everything in me not to chuckle—his comment was exactly what I would have said in response to that question—but I remained serious. "Will I ever see you again?" I asked.

He studied me, and I could tell he was thinking carefully about his response. "Yes," he finally said. "You can count on it."

Then he hurried across the room and thrust himself out of the window, moving so fast that I didn't have time to tell him to be careful.

By the time I looked out to make sure he'd gotten down safely, he was gone.

# 23

# JACEN

I SPED through the outskirts of the village, as far as I could go without crossing the boundary of the Vale. It had been so long since I'd run free like this, and it felt *good*.

It allowed me to think. Mainly about Annika.

Why hadn't my compulsion worked on her?

Perhaps I was so spellbound in her presence that I hadn't been able to focus enough while compelling her? I supposed that would make sense… except that I'd felt the magic rushing through my system as I'd spoken. The compulsion *should* have worked. I may not have been a vampire for long, but I knew that.

I also knew that she couldn't be immune to compulsion. The only creatures on Earth who were immune were the original vampires and the vampires they'd sired. And I was positive that Annika wasn't either of those.

She must have been lying about the wormwood.

That was why I'd promised we would see each other again—because I planned on figuring out a way to get her to remove whatever wormwood talisman she wore, and then I would successfully compel her to forget me.

Otherwise, she would eventually find out who I was. After all, Laila wasn't going to keep me locked in the palace forever. And if she was serious about finding me a bride and making a giant spectacle of it, all of the humans in the village would soon see the face of their new vampire prince. Including Annika.

I didn't want her to know I'd lied to her. But more importantly, I didn't want her to try convincing me to turn her. Because after hearing her speak with such conviction about how much she wished to be a vampire, I had a feeling that nothing short of death would stop her from trying to get what she wanted.

Also, I *wanted* to see Annika again. She made me feel more alive than I'd felt since being turned into a vampire, and I didn't want to lose that feeling.

"Jacen?" someone called from nearby, stopping me in my tracks.

I turned around and saw Daniel, my main guard. He was joined by Zachary and Elijah—they'd been three of the guards who had appeared at the Christmas Eve celebration at the village.

They surrounded me, waiting for an explanation.

"The three of you never saw me here," I told them, feeling the magic of compulsion flow through my body and out of my voice. "Now, run back to the palace and let me be on my way."

"Not going to work this time." Daniel pulled a chain necklace out from under his shirt—dangling from it was a clear gem with a green plant sealed inside. Wormwood.

The other two pulled out necklaces of their own, revealing matching talismans.

"Queen Laila's not going to be happy when she finds out you're wearing those," I said.

"Doubtful." Daniel smirked. "Seeing that she gave them to us and ordered us to find you."

"So she knows I'm gone?" I asked, although the better question was if she knew how many people I'd compelled on my way out.

"She does," Daniel said, and the three of them stepped closer, the threat clear. Do what they asked, or fight. "And she's waiting in the palace to see you."

# 24

# JACEN

SURE ENOUGH, Laila was sitting in her office, typing so fast on her laptop that the clicking of the keys whizzed together.

"Jacen." She lowered the screen and smiled at me. "I heard you had a little adventure tonight." Then she looked at the guards, holding out a hand to them. "But before we hear about it—the stones."

They removed the necklaces and handed them to her.

"Thank you," she said. "Now, where were we? Oh yes—Jacen's adventure. Please, tell me what happened." She dropped the necklaces onto her desk and leaned back in her chair, making herself comfortable. "I do *love* a good story."

And so, I told her everything.

Except for meeting Annika and escaping with her from the square to hide in the attic of the Tavern.

According to *my* story, I'd hung out at the square, observing the humans there, and left after spotting the guards. I'd made my way to the edge of the village and spent some time in the forest near the boundary of the Vale before returning to the palace, which was where the guards had found me.

Laila's eyes twinkled as she listened. "*Very* interesting," she said once I was done. "Guards—you can leave now. Thank you for doing your duty and bringing Prince Jacen back home."

They nodded and left the room.

Once they were gone, she stared at me for a few seconds, saying nothing.

It took all my willpower to stop myself from fidgeting under her gaze, but I stayed strong. She might be a centuries year old vampire queen, but I would *not* let her intimidate me.

The only thing Laila hated more than disobedience was weakness.

"Impressive," she finally said, and I blinked, unsure if I'd heard correctly.

"Excuse me?" I asked.

"You heard me," she said. "I was wondering how much longer you were going to accept being kept inside the palace walls. If you'd waited a few weeks longer to attempt escape, I would have started to question my decision to turn you into a vampire prince. After all, a complacent prince is a boring prince, don't you think?"

"Seriously?" I said, my tone laced with anger. "This was all some kind of twisted test?"

"Of course." She smiled. "And you passed. With flying colors, I might add, since as far as I'm aware, no humans were harmed during your adventure. Congratulations."

I assumed she wanted me to thank her, but I refused to give her the pleasure. "Will I now be allowed to roam the Vale as I please?" I asked instead.

"Soon," she said, tapping her fingers on the desk. "But first, we need to present you to the kingdom."

"What do you mean?" I asked, although I was secretly glad she hadn't brought up the topic of wanting me to find a bride again.

"You're hardly the first potential vampire prince that I've turned," she said with a musical laugh. "Throughout the centuries, I've identified many human specimens who had potential to become princes of the Vale."

"Such as Scott and Alexander," I said, naming the "brothers" who I'd barely spoken to during my time in the palace.

"Of course," she said. "Haven't you wondered why

they haven't made much of an effort to get to know you? You are *brothers* after all."

"They worried I would take my own life because I couldn't handle the transition," I said curtly. "Like many others have before me."

"You're only partially correct." She brought her hair over her shoulders and smiled, as if preparing for another revelation. "It's true that many humans I've turned have taken their own lives. But there are other ways they've been eliminated."

"What sort of ways?" I asked, since that was the only one I'd heard of thus far.

"Only the strongest humans come close to qualifying to being turned into a vampire prince," she said. "And, as you also know—from your own experience—the stronger a vampire is, the harder it is to control the bloodlust."

"And?" I asked, since she wasn't telling me anything I didn't already know.

"We cannot have a prince of the Vale who's unable to control his bloodlust."

"So what?" I asked, but then I paused, realization dawning on me. "If I hadn't gotten control of my bloodlust, you were going to kill me," I said, having a dreadful feeling that I was correct.

Her pause confirmed my suspicion.

The only thing keeping me from attempting to

strangle her right there was knowing that she was one of the strongest vampires in the world, with centuries of fighting experience, and that if I tried anything her guards would be here in a second.

"Like I said, it would be unacceptable to have a prince of the Vale who was unable to control his bloodlust," she repeated. "I nearly ended you after your attack on the village. But it was the first time one of my princes made it past the guards and to the village, and it was so soon after your transition. You held so much *promise* that I simply couldn't allow it. No—I had to see if you lived up to your potential. Even if just to satiate my own curiosity."

"How many others have there been?" I asked, refusing to give into her obvious attempt at goading me to thank her for letting me live.

"Between you and Alexander?" she asked, since he was the youngest of my two "brothers." "A few. They all went mad from the bloodlust. Once they reached the point of no return, if they didn't kill themselves I had the guards take care of it for them. Or, if they were taking so long to adjust to the bloodlust that it was clear they would never get control over themselves, I had them taken care of as well. But this past week—by proving you're able to control yourself while feeding on humans, by mastering compulsion to escape the palace, *and* by not murdering any humans while you were out in the village—you've proven yourself a worthy prince. Finally."

"So you're not going to kill me," I said, my voice hollow.

"Not anytime soon." She chuckled.

I stood completely still, more on guard than ever. If I didn't realize it earlier, I now had no doubt—Laila had no humanity left in her.

If she ever had any at all.

"Relax," she said, and she stood up, walking around her desk to face me. "You're about to become an official prince of the Vale. I expected you to be happy to hear the news."

"I would be," I said through gritted teeth. "But you still haven't brought up your previous request for me to find a bride, and I know it isn't because you've forgotten. And as an *official* prince, I would like to have more say in who I marry and when."

"Oh, you will *definitely* still be choosing a bride, and soon." She narrowed her eyes, as if daring me to challenge her. When I didn't give into the bait, she continued, "But first things first. Because in one week, we'll throw a party to officially present you to kingdom. Afterward, you'll be able to roam the Vale as you please."

I should have been rejoicing. After all, she was

giving me what I'd wanted—freedom from the palace walls.

But all I could do was wonder what Annika's reaction would be when she realized who I truly was. Which only gave me more incentive to get her to admit to having wormwood, and having her remove it so I could compel her to forget me.

And now I only had one week to get it done.

## 25

## CAMELIA

I SAT on my bed in my room, hunched over the seeing crystal that the human boy had snatched in his failed mission to the Crystal Cavern. Each day the visions I saw in the crystal were becoming more and more clear.

I knew by now that the person who could successfully free Geneva was a girl. The crystal had shown her to me from a distance, or from behind, or as blurred image—but I still hadn't gotten a clear view of her face. All I knew was that she was pale, short, and slender, with dark brown hair... and that she lived in the human village. But I couldn't exactly order *every* human who lived there to attempt to enter the Crystal Cavern. No —I needed to know precisely who I was searching for.

I also knew that whoever she was, she stole food from vampires. I'd seen it in the crystal. It appalled me that a *thief* was destined to obtain Geneva's sapphire ring, but what would be would be. And I supposed it was a good thing, in the long run. Her criminal activities would provide the perfect reason to capture her and get her to do my bidding.

But first, I needed to see exactly *who* she was.

I'd been resting my magic as much as possible for the past few days—as much as I could, given that it was my responsibility to keep the boundary around the Vale. But I *had* been lessening the magic I'd been using on temperature control. A few older humans hadn't survived because of it, but oh well—the sacrifices were worth it for the possibility of freeing Geneva.

Especially because the rest made it so my magic felt stronger today than it had been in a long time.

And so, I gazed into the crystal and said, "Show me the face of the one who can enter the Crystal Cavern and free Geneva."

An image started to form in the crystal, blurry at first, but soon it sharpened around the edges. I saw a room—no, a crawlspace—with bookshelves and blankets and a tiny window. Below the window was a blurry form of the girl.

I dug deep into my magic, forcing it to rise within me and throwing all of it at the crystal. As I did, the scene sharpened from the outward in, and the shape of the girl finally became clear.

I gasped upon seeing her face. Because she was the girl who'd been with the boy the night he'd killed the wolf in the village.

I didn't know her name, but I knew where to find her—at the pathetic little bar that the humans called the Tavern.

# 26

## ANNIKA

I SERVED a Tavern customer one of the standard fares—beans with rice, and a pint of cheap beer—unable to keep myself from looking over my shoulder every couple of seconds. I couldn't explain it, but I hadn't been able to get rid of the feeling that someone was watching me.

It had started soon after Mike left for his job in the palace, and it was growing stronger and stronger each day. Even while I was alone reading.

I chalked it up to the fact that it was my first time since being kidnapped that Mike hadn't been around to look out for me. Each day he was gone, I got more and more worried about where he was and what he was doing.

Now, on top of that, there was Jake.

After Jake had left last night, I'd climbed out of the window and came inside normally. The Tavern had been nearly empty since most people in the village had still been out partying. I'd gone to sleep before they'd returned.

But Jake was so strange and mysterious, and since he'd left, I hadn't been able to get him off my mind. I was like an elementary school girl with a crush.

I hated how vulnerable it made me feel.

"Has everything been okay with you recently?" Tanya asked as I returned to my spot with her behind the bar. The lunch crowd had just finished up, so we busied ourselves by cleaning glasses.

"Yeah." I forced a smile, but it felt fake, and I knew she could see through it.

"Are you sure?" she asked, softer now. "Because if you need to talk, you know I'm here for you, right?"

"I know." I glanced around, but there were no new customers, and the ones I'd just served were taking their time with their meals. And Tanya *did* want to genuinely help.

Maybe it would be good to talk with her.

"I'm worried about Mike," I started. "He's been gone for so long, and I don't know." I shrugged. "Something doesn't feel right."

"How long did the witch make it sound like he'd be gone for?" Tanya asked.

"She didn't give a specific time frame," I said. "But I assumed he would be back by now. It's been nearly a month... I thought we would have at least *heard* from him."

"If this job in the palace is as secret as it sounds, the vampires probably aren't letting him contact us," she said. "But he'll be back soon. He wouldn't leave us all here on our own forever."

"I hope so." I sighed and focused on cleaning the rim of a beer mug. The more days that passed, the worse I felt for not encouraging him to take more time to think about the offer.

"Hey." Tanya placed her glass down and looked at me. "Mike's tough. And his family's been in the Vale for generations—he knows how to handle himself around vampires. He'll be fine."

"Of course he will be," I said, as if saying it out loud could make it true.

"Worrying won't change anything," Tanya said. "So let's talk about things you *do* have control over."

"Like what?" I asked.

"Like that mysterious guy you danced with at the Christmas party last night," she said, a mischievous glint crossing her eyes.

Heat rose to my cheeks, and I picked up another mug, even though it was already clean. "What about him?" I asked, trying to sound casual.

"Where did you guys go?" she asked. "One second you were dancing with him, then the vampires showed up, and you were gone."

"Why *did* the vampires show up?" I asked, since it had been nagging me since last night. If I knew why they'd showed up, maybe I would have a better understanding about why Jake needed to get away from them.

"They were checking to make sure we were all safe," she told me. "They walked around the party for a bit and then they left."

"That's it?" I asked.

"Yeah." She nodded.

"Weird."

She leaned closer to me, looked around the bar as if checking to make sure no one was listening, and lowered her voice. "A lot of people think it has to do with the wolves," she said. "Everyone's been on edge since the attack."

"Did another one get in?" I asked.

"Not that I know of," she said. "But after what happened, it makes sense to heighten security."

"I suppose it does," I said, although it hardly explained why Jake had such an intense desire to not be seen by the vampires. Something more was going on... and next time I saw him, I intended on finding out what it was.

"So, what happened with the guy?" she returned to the original subject. "Where did you two *go* all night?"

I couldn't tell her the real reason we'd needed to leave, but she wasn't going to rest unless I told her *something,* so I searched my mind for a plausible explanation. "We went for a walk," I said, since it wasn't a total lie.

"And…?" She raised an eyebrow, waiting for me to continue.

"We talked," I said.

"Did you kiss?"

I laughed, because of *course* that was what Tanya wanted to know. She'd probably been planning on asking since we'd started our shift.

"Is that a yes?" She brightened.

"No." I frowned, since I'd *wanted* him to kiss me. At one point I'd thought he was going to… but instead he'd told me to forget we ever met.

It was so confusing.

I wanted to confide to Tanya about it—to get advice—but I couldn't do that without telling her the truth of what had happened last night. And I didn't want to get her tangled up in whatever trouble Jake might be involved in. I also didn't want to betray his trust.

"Really?" she asked. "You were out with him for hours and you didn't even kiss?"

"No." There were no more glasses that needed

cleaning, so I turned around and wiped down the back counter instead.

"But you *wanted* to kiss him," she said, continuing before I could answer. "Are you going to see him again?"

I paused, not sure what to say. That was the same question I'd been wondering since last night. He'd gone from wanting me to forget him to promising we would see each other again, so I wasn't sure *what* to believe.

I wanted to believe we would see each other again.

But who knew what would happen? I especially hated that even though it hadn't been twenty-four hours since we'd met, my time with Jake felt like a dream that I would never be able to get a proper hold of again.

"Well, I guess we have your answer," Tanya said, amusement filling her tone.

"What do you mean?" I asked.

"You'll never guess who just walked through the door."

# 27

# JACEN

SHE WAS the first person I saw when I entered the Tavern.

Her back was toward me, and despite her hair being pulled into a ponytail, I would have recognized her anywhere.

She quickly turned around, dropping her arms to her sides when her eyes met mine.

I'd spent all morning thinking about how to remove the wormwood she carried on her so I could compel her to forget me. And so, once coming up with a semblance of a plan, I'd put on the same jacket I'd worn last night—pulling the hood over my head to avoid recognition—and had headed out of the palace. It was a relief to not have to sneak around, since I could now come and go as I pleased. No one even asked where I was going. I was grateful to have the freedom I'd longed for since being taken here, but at the same time, it felt strange—like I was doing something wrong, even though I knew I wasn't.

The only thing that felt wrong was knowing that soon, Annika's memories of me would be erased—that she would only know me as a vampire prince of the Vale. As a stranger to be feared.

I walked up to the bar, my gaze locked on hers. "Annika," I said once I was standing in front of her.

Her blonde friend muttered something about checking on the customers and hurried around the bar, leaving us alone.

"Jake." Annika spoke my name—my *fake* name—with as much curiosity and intrigue as I'd said hers. Then she glanced around and tightened her ponytail, apparently remembering where we were. "Would you like a drink?" she asked me.

"No," I said. "I want to talk to you. Alone."

"I'm working," she told me, her eyes suspicious. "But I suppose I can take a break for a bit… if Tanya doesn't mind."

Her blonde friend—Tanya—conveniently chose that moment to hop back behind the bar. "Of course I don't mind," she said with a smile. "It's always slow around this time of night, anyway. I've got it covered." She looked back and forth between me and Annika, clearly excited for what was about to happen.

Before being kidnapped to the Vale, I guessed that Tanya was the type of girl who loved to gossip.

Once I was able to compel Annika to forget me, it looked like I was going to have to compel Tanya to forget me, too.

Or I could compel Tanya right now. It would be a good test to see if she had wormwood on her as well. I guessed she did. After all, the most likely place for Annika to have gotten the wormwood was through the place where she worked and lived.

"Annika and I are going to go," I told Tanya, meeting her eyes and filling my voice with the magic of compulsion. "Once we're gone, you're going to forget you ever met me."

Her eyes dilated slightly—so slightly that a human wouldn't have noticed—and she nodded.

The compulsion had worked.

# 28

# JACEN

"What was that about?" Annika asked the moment we stepped into the alley behind the restaurant.

"What was what about?" I asked her.

"You told Tanya to forget she ever met you."

"I did." I nodded, and then I put the magic into my voice again, just in case she didn't have wormwood on her today. "And you're going to forget me as well."

"I already told you I won't do that." She crossed her arms, narrowing her eyes. "I don't believe you want me to do that either."

"Really?" I asked, unable to hide the amusement from my tone. "And why's that?"

"Because if you wanted nothing to do with me, you wouldn't be here right now."

"I suppose not," I said, since she would be right—if I were a human.

"And you wanted to get out of the town square so quickly after the vampires showed up last night," she continued, watching me carefully as she spoke. "As if you thought they were looking for you."

"Why would they be looking for me?" I asked, since I'd always found that the best way to avoid answering a question was to respond with another question.

"That's what I've been thinking about since you left last night," she said. "It doesn't make sense. Unless..."

"Unless what?" I asked, curious to hear her theories. Even if she guessed correctly, I wouldn't tell her, of course. But it would be interesting to hear her ideas.

She paused, as if wondering if she should continue.

"Go on," I told her. "I want to know."

"It's just a thought, and I'm probably completely wrong," she started. "But... wolves have been getting past the boundary and into the Vale."

"I've heard that." I nodded, since of course I was well aware of what had been happening—and also aware of the limited information given to the humans. "But it was only one wolf. And the vampires quickly took care of it."

"You believe that?" She chuckled and shook her head, as if she found the story ridiculous.

"Don't you?" I asked.

"Partly," she said, and before I could ask what part, she continued. "But I think the wolves are becoming more of a problem than the vampires are letting on."

"The vampires are stronger than the wolves," I told her. "They have them under control."

"That's what they *want* us to think," she said.

"Okay," I said, intrigued about where she might be going with this. "So… what do you think the wolves have to do with me wanting to leave the square last night?"

"The wolves are shifters," she started. "They can change into human form."

"They only change when necessary," I told her. "They prefer being in wolf form."

Her eyes lit up, and I worried that I'd said too much. "How do you know so much about wolves?" she asked.

"People talk." I shrugged. "*We* might be new to the Vale, but some of the human families have been here for generations. They talk, and I listen."

"That's all?" She raised an eyebrow.

"It is." The lie tasted bitter on my lips. I hated lying to her, but I couldn't let her get even *more* suspicious of me. "What more do you think is going on?" I asked.

"I think the wolves are trying to infiltrate the Vale." She stood straighter, as if challenging me to tell her otherwise. "I think that at least one of them got in last night, and that the vampires were searching for him."

"Interesting theory," I said. "But if a wolf got in, surely there would have been an attack on the humans —on us?" I added, catching myself at the last second.

"Let me finish." She held a hand up, and I was silent. "Let's say a wolf got in, and they were there for some sort of bigger plan," she continued. "If that wolf saw the vampires, he would want to get as far away from them as possible. And I'd never seen you *anywhere* in the village before yesterday—no one had. You came out of nowhere... or from the forests outside of the boundary."

"Back up," I told her, barely suppressing my laughter. "You're not implying that I'm a wolf... are you?"

"That's exactly what I'm implying," she said.

I couldn't help myself any longer—I laughed.

"What?" She placed her hands on her hips, glaring at me. "What's so funny?"

"I'm not a wolf." I shook my head, still amused by her accusation. "Your theory was interesting, but you're entirely off base."

"Fine." She stepped closer, watching me in challenge. "Let's say I believe you."

"Let's." I nodded, waiting for her to continue.

"If you're not a wolf, then why did you run from the vampires last night?" she asked. "And why are you here now?"

I kept my eyes locked on hers, not wanting to back

down from her challenge. Electricity buzzed over every inch of my skin at the intensity of her gaze. My senses went on overdrive, and I was hit with an awareness of the blood pounding through her veins, the sweet scent of it making my fangs ache in my gums.

But I clenched my fists, controlling the urge to drink from her. Luckily I'd thought to feed before coming here. If I hadn't...

I shook my head, not letting myself contemplate it further. Thinking about it would only make the urge to taste her blood stronger.

Instead I thought about how to answer her question. She was looking at me with so much hope—so much *trust*. Suddenly, I stopped wanting to taste her blood.

I wanted to kiss her instead.

Would she be looking at me like that if she knew what I truly was? Or would she think I was a monster?

After what she'd told me last night—about how she wanted to become a vampire—I didn't know. But it didn't matter. Because turning her wasn't an option. Even if she survived the change, Laila would kill her for being turned without permission. She would never have her chance to escape the Vale.

Turning her would be condemning her to death.

Which was why I needed to stop thinking about pushing her up against the wall and crushing my lips to hers. I needed to remember why I was here—to have her remove her wormwood charm so I could compel her to forget me.

But if I flat out asked if she had access to wormwood, she would think I was using her for the plant. And that wouldn't be true. Because in a different world —a world where we were both human and unaware of the existence of vampires, witches, wolves, and all other supernaturals—I would have wanted to get to know her better. I would have asked her out on a date.

I definitely would have already kissed her.

But that world had been erased for both of us when we'd been taken here. We would never get it back.

There was no point in pining for what I'd lost.

Really, there was no point in worrying about hurting her feelings by asking her about the wormwood, either. Because soon I would compel her to forget me, and she would forget everything we ever did and all the conversations we ever had.

Whatever I said and did until then was irrelevant, because to her, it would all be erased.

"Well?" She crossed her arms, irritation crossing her eyes. "Are you just going to keep staring at me, or are you going to answer my question?"

"Your question…" I trailed, my thoughts having deviated so much that I'd forgotten what we'd been discussing.

"About why you're here?"

"Right. That." I swallowed and realized—to hell with it. I was just going to compel her anyway. She was going to forget everything, so until then, I might as well do I what I wanted. "I'm here for this."

Before she could ask what I meant, I pinned her against the wall and crushed my lips to hers, losing myself in her kiss.

# 29

# ANNIKA

KISSING JAKE FELT as natural as breathing.

Everything in that moment felt right—the way our bodies curved together, the pressure of his lips, and the thrill that ran up my spine as his tongue brushed against mine. All the anger from fighting earlier morphed into passion, and I pulled him closer, never wanting the kiss to end.

Even if he *was* a wolf—which I still suspected he might be—I didn't care. Clearly he'd never intended to hurt me. If he had, he would have already. All I cared about was that right now, he wanted me as much as I wanted him.

This was the best thing that had happened to me since being kidnapped to the Vale, and I intended to enjoy every second of it.

Suddenly the back door of the Tavern swung open, and I pulled away from Jake, my heart leaping into my throat at the prospect of one of the other workers barging in on such an intimate moment.

But it wasn't one of my friends that I saw.

It was vampires.

Five of them, dressed in the sleek black outfits of the vampire guard, their mouths open to bare their fangs.

Jake's back was toward them—he had no idea that they were vampires and not humans. But he pulled his hood back on, clearly still having something to hide—and started to glance over his shoulder to check on our visitors.

"Don't," I said under my breath, keeping my hand in his and stopping him from looking at them.

They had to be here for him. We needed to run.

But what way out was there? My eyes darted around the alley, but we were at a dead end. There were only two ways out—the back door to the Tavern, and the path that led to the street. Both were blocked by vampires. We *might* be able to climb the wall, but while I was fast, the vampires were faster. It was impossible for humans to outrun vampires.

It was especially impossible for humans to fight them.

We were trapped.

Jake turned around, and I stepped forward to stand

in front of him, not wanting the vampires to see his face. Luckily this alleyway was poorly lit, and his hood was drawn so low over his eyes that his features were covered with the shadows.

"Don't bother trying to escape," the vampire in front said, his gaze locked on mine. He looked Scandinavian —tall and blond, with light blue eyes.

He was the vampire who had killed my mom. Rage filled my body at the sight of him—I wanted to kill him. But I knew I couldn't. So I just stood there, hating myself for being so weak. For being so *human*.

"We don't want to hurt you," he continued." We *can't* hurt you, actually—we were ordered not to. So if you'll just come with us, we can be on our way."

"Me?" I asked, my voice squeaking.

"You're Annika, correct?" He watched me, ignoring Jake completely. "You were with the human boy Mike on the day that Camelia chose him for a job at the palace?"

"You know Mike?" I stepped forward, hope surging in my chest at the prospect of hearing news about my friend. "How is he? Is he okay? When will he be back?"

"Your friend is dead," the vampire behind him spoke. "And if you don't come with us, you will be too."

"No." I shook my head and stepped back, straight into Jake's arms.

He held me tightly, as if ready to stop me from lashing out.

"He can't be dead," I said. "You're lying."

"Why would we lie?" The leader glared at the vampire who'd said it, as if mentally telling him to shut up. "My soldier speaks the truth about your friend. But Camelia has instructed us to take you unharmed, so that's what we'll do. And you won't fight us if you know what's good for you."

"No," I said again, my thoughts swirling at a million miles a second. Mike couldn't be dead. He *couldn't* be.

Except he *could* be. Camelia had said he would be back soon. Yet it had been almost a month. He'd made no effort to contact anyone at the Tavern to let us know how he was. He hadn't even sent a letter.

I think I'd known for a while that he was gone. I just hadn't wanted to face the truth.

"You're coming with us." The leader smiled, revealing the entirety of his fangs.

I wanted to say no—that I *wouldn't* go with them. But I knew better. They were five vampires and we were two humans. I might be quick, but I was nowhere near as fast as a vampire.

I was weak and helpless. Just like I'd been a year ago when I'd watched him kill my mom.

As a human in a world of supernaturals, I would *always* be helpless.

I was going to be taken. Jake was going to be taken.

And there was nothing we could do to stop it.

# 30

# JACEN

At first I'd assumed the guards were there for me.

If it hadn't been for Annika, I would have bolted. But I would never leave her alone with those monsters. And if I picked her up and carried her, I wouldn't be able to outrun them. I was strong, but strong enough to fight off five vampire guards *and* make sure Annika was safe?

I couldn't risk her life like that.

I also couldn't let them take her.

Which left only one viable option.

"Stop." Magic filled my tone, and I pulled my hood down, staring at each of the vampires. I recognized them all—I'd recognized them the moment they'd walked out of that door.

Their eyes widened when they saw me.

"Prince Jacen." Daniel gasped, and he and the others pulled themselves together. "What are you…?" He looked back and forth from me to Annika, as if trying to figure out why I was there.

"Prince?" Annika repeated, looking up at me in question.

I couldn't bring myself to meet her gaze. I couldn't imagine how betrayed she must feel.

She deserved answers, but for her safety I first had to deal with the vampires who'd been sent to bring her to the palace.

"Why I'm here doesn't concern you," I told Daniel, throwing as much magic into my voice as possible. "Who sent you?"

"Camelia." He swallowed, and added, "Sir."

"Why?"

"To fetch the girl." He glanced at Annika. "Unharmed."

"Did she say *why* she needed you to 'fetch' Annika?" I asked.

"No, sir." He shook his head. "She didn't even know the girl's name. She just said to find a girl who worked at the Tavern—she gave us her description and said she was friends with a boy named Mike. Once inside, we asked the girl at the bar who fit that description. She said Annika's name and told us she went this way. She did, however, fail to mention a companion."

"Tanya," Annika muttered, her voice laced with hurt.

"She's only a human," I told her, meaning it as comfort. "She *had* to answer the vampires' questions. It was that or have the answer beaten out of her. She had no choice."

Annika glared at me and pulled her hand out of mine, her eyes shining with distrust.

I was going to have a *lot* of groveling to do after I finished saving her life. But for now, I turned back to Daniel, since I needed to get as much information from him as possible to help Annika.

"Do *any* of you know why Camelia asked for Annika?" I looked at all of the vampires—men who had guarded me and kept me company while I was trapped in the palace—forcing as much compulsion into my voice as possible. Their pupils were all dilated, their stances more relaxed—the magic was working. "Did she give any hint at all?"

"No," they all repeated.

"Only that she wanted the girl unharmed," Daniel said again. "Beyond that, we know nothing."

"Fine," I said, since this was getting us nowhere, and the more time we lost, the more danger Annika was in. "Avoid returning to Camelia for as long as you're able. Avoid returning to *anyone* who knows you're on this mission. Tell no one that you saw me—or Annika."

"Understood." Daniel nodded, and as quickly as a

human could blink, he and the other vampires were gone from the alley.

Annika also attempted to run, but I reached for her arm, stopping her.

Did she truly believe she could outrun a vampire?

She glared at me, her eyes filled with challenge. "Let me go," she commanded. "*Prince* Jacen."

"No," I told her. "I've compelled them to leave, but Camelia's smart. It won't be long until she realizes what I've done and sends more vampires to find us—this time with wormwood to make sure I can't compel them. We need to get out of here while we still can."

"Are you serious?" She tried to pull out of my grip, but given the differences in our strength, her attempt was futile. "I don't know what kind of game you're playing, but I don't want any part of it."

"I'm not playing a game." I took a deep breath, trying to be as patient as possible. "I'm on your side here."

"You seriously expect me to believe you?" she asked. "You—a vampire prince who pretended to be a human so he could use me for his own amusement? I can't believe I actually *fell* for it. I feel like such an idiot."

"You're not an idiot," I said quickly. "And it wasn't like that—not at all."

"Really?" She narrowed her eyes. "So tell me, Your Highness. What *was* it like?"

"It's a long story," I told her. "And I'll tell you all of it —once we're out of here."

She held her gaze stubbornly with mine. "You better tell me some of it, or I'm not going anywhere with you."

I chuckled, because given the differences in our strength, did she really think she had a choice?

I hated thinking that, because she *deserved* a choice. But if I left her here it wouldn't be long until Camelia found her again and took her to the palace.

Once she was in the palace, she was as good as dead.

"A little over a year ago, I was turned into a vampire against my will," I said quickly. "I've lived in the palace since then—I know what happens to the humans who are brought there. And I will *not* let that happen to you. So come with me. Please. I'll do everything I can to bring you to safety."

For a moment, fear crossed over her face, and I was grateful that she realized how much was at stake here. But a second later, her expression switched back to hard resolve and firm determination.

She might be a human and I a vampire, but I swear her mind was just as strong as mine—if not stronger.

"Why did you lie to me?" she finally asked. "About who you are."

"Like I said, I was turned into a vampire against my will," I repeated. "Last night, all I wanted was to feel normal. To feel *human*. That was all it was supposed to be—one night. I never expected to meet you, or for us to spend hours together and have the connection we did. More than anything, I never wanted to hurt you."

"Is that why you came to talk to me today?" she asked. "To tell me the truth?"

I wanted to lie to her—to say yes. But I couldn't. Not after already having lied so much.

"No," I said. "I came because I couldn't stop thinking about you. I may have lied about who I am—about *what* I am—but my feelings for you are real. So please, Annika—come with me. Let me save your life."

# 31

# ANNIKA

I HAD no reason to trust him. Not after he'd lied about so much.

How had everything changed so fast?

Mike was dead. Jake—*Jacen*—was a vampire prince. Camelia had sent vampire guards to bring me to the palace. Tanya had told them where I was without even trying to protect me.

It was too much to take in at once.

But I knew one thing for sure—those vampire guards would be back. As a human, I was powerless to stop them. They would drag me to the palace and do who knows what to me. I would likely end up dead.

And here was Jacen, offering to save my life.

The strangest thing was, despite his lying to me, I

*did* trust him. At least with this. After all, he could have killed me in this alley. He could have tasted my blood. Instead, he'd kissed me. I'd kissed him back.

Part of my mind knew that spending a few hours talking with him last night and kissing him today wasn't enough to earn trust—especially after he'd lied about so much.

But if I didn't trust him now, I was as good as dead.

"Fine," I said, since I was out of any other feasible option. "Let's go."

He nodded, and moving so quickly that he was a blur, picked me up and placed me on his back. "Hold on tight," he said, and I wrapped my arms around his neck. "Tighter," he instructed. "You won't hurt me."

"Have you ever done this before?" I asked.

"I've seen it done," he said simply. "Now, you might want to close your eyes."

The next thing I knew, he was zipping through the back streets of the village, zigzagging to avoid crashing into the occasional human in the path. The wind whipped across my face with so much force that tears streamed from my eyes. The speed reminded me of when I went on a vacation with my family to St. Kitts and my brother and I went on a banana boat ride behind a speedboat. Grant kept telling the driver to go faster and faster, until it got so difficult to hold on that we both went flying off.

Luckily, Jacen ran a lot steadier than that, so it wasn't nearly as difficult to hold on. But more unnerving than the speed was knowing that if a human were running this fast, they surely would have crashed into something by now.

Apparently, vampires had much better reflexes than humans could ever imagine.

Soon enough, we were out of the village and tearing through the wilderness. We were higher up in the mountains now—so high that the ground was covered in snow.

There was only one other time I'd ventured this far out of the village—when I'd tried to escape and had gotten attacked by that wolf.

"Wait," I said, barely able to catch my breath as the wind whipped past me.

He slowed down to a stop, the snow skidding under his feet. "What?" he asked.

"Where are we going?"

"We're leaving," he said quickly, angling his head so his cheek brushed mine. "We have to get you out of here. It's the only way to keep you safe."

"Leaving the *Vale*?" I asked, unsure if I'd understood correctly. Because we couldn't just leave the Vale.

Could we?

"Yes." He turned back around, but before he could continue running, I untangled myself from his neck and jumped down to stand. My legs shook when I landed—apparently I'd been holding on to him tighter than I'd realized.

"What are you doing?" He turned to me, irritation crossing his face.

"We can't just *leave,*" I pointed out.

"I thought that was what you wanted?" His expression shifted from irritation to confusion. "Freedom from life as a blood slave?"

"Yes," I said, although we both knew that wasn't all I wanted—I would never be safe from the vampires as long as I remained human. "But what about the wolves?"

"I'm a vampire prince." He brushed away my question. "The wolves won't attack me. Or you, if I ask them not to."

"Okay," I said, although given the fact that the wolves had been breaking into the Vale and attacking humans, I doubted the relationship between the vampires and wolves was as solid as he was making it out to be. "But let's say we *do* make it past the wolves. It's winter in Canada. I'll freeze to death before we make it to the nearest town—wherever that might be." I motioned to the flimsy clothes I was wearing—jeans and a long sleeved t-shirt—to prove my point. The temperature in the Vale was regulated by the witch—by

Camelia. Once we left, we would enter the full onslaught of the Canadian winter.

"Good point," he said, his eyes roaming over my thin clothing. Then he took a deep breath and lifted his wrist to his mouth, puncturing his skin with his fangs. "Here," he said, holding his bleeding wrist out to me. "Drink."

"What?" I widened my eyes and stepped back. "You're turning me into a vampire? What about everything you told me about the transition—how not everyone lives? And how any vampire turned illegally is killed?"

"Drinking my blood won't turn you into a vampire." He chuckled, his eyes dark. "The process is a bit more complicated than that."

"Oh," I said, my stomach dropping with disappointment. Because despite the challenges, I supposed I was hoping he was giving me what I wanted—the chance to become a vampire and never be helpless again. After all, even now that he was trying to help me, I was still at his mercy. As long as I remained a human, I would never be truly safe. "So if drinking your blood won't turn me into a vampire, then what *will* it do?" I asked.

"You don't know?" He looked surprised.

I rolled my eyes. "If I knew, would I be asking?"

He was silent for a few seconds, as if contemplating how to begin. "I suppose the power of vampire blood is kept from the humans in the Vale for a good reason," he started. "Like wormwood, it could be used against them. And you know all about that, clearly, since you have it on you now."

"What?" I scrunched my eyebrows, getting more and more confused by the second. "I don't have wormwood on me."

"You're lying," he said stiffly.

"I'm absolutely not." I didn't get it—why would he think I had wormwood on me?

He studied me, as if waiting for me to claim otherwise, but I had nothing to confess.

"What happens when a human drinks vampire blood?" I asked instead, bringing him back to the previous subject.

"If the humans knew, they might attempt to rebel," he said slowly. "But this knowledge will keep you safe, so I'll tell you."

"Okay." I waited, noticing that the puncture marks on his wrist had stopped bleeding and were beginning to heal.

"If a human drinks the blood of a vampire, they'll have the abilities of a vampire for twenty-four hours," he said. "Speed, healing, strength… they'll even be able to drink blood themselves, despite not actually needing it to survive. But more importantly, drinking vampire blood will stop you from freezing to death once we cross the boundary of the Vale."

"So I'll sort of become a vampire," I said.

"Yes." He nodded. "Temporarily."

"And what's the process to turn a human into a vampire?" I asked. "*Not* temporarily?"

"We're not discussing that," he said, his eyes hard. "There's no time. Besides, I will not turn you—or any human, for that matter—into a vampire."

"What if it's what I want?" I was challenging him, but from the way he was staring at me, I knew he wouldn't back down. At least not right now.

"The change might kill you," he said. "Or drive you to kill yourself."

"I'm willing to take that risk." I raised my chin, not backing down. "I would rather be dead than a victim for the rest of my life."

"It's more than that." He sighed and ran his hand through his hair. "Do you believe in an afterlife, Annika?"

"I don't know." I backed away, surprised by his sudden change of subject. "Maybe."

"Well, I do," he said. "As a human I was far from perfect, but I never did anything that would doom me to Hell. As a vampire..." Darkness passed over his eyes, like clouds over twin moons. "No vampire who survives the transition is able to control their bloodlust enough at first to stop them from killing. We're murderers—all of us. Is that the sort of creature you want to become? A *monster*?"

I gulped, frightened by his confession. Because no, of course I didn't want to kill.

But I didn't want to be a weak human for the rest of my life, either.

"I wouldn't let myself be around a human until I could control it." I straightened my shoulders, not wanting him to doubt me. "And I *would* control it. I would learn how to do it."

"How would you know you could control it without testing it on a human?" He smiled, showing me his fangs. For the first time since discovering what he was, it sunk in that he'd killed before. I knew I should feel scared of him… but I didn't. Because I trusted he wouldn't hurt me.

I pressed my lips together, because he had a good point. "I would test it on someone who deserved it," I said. "On a murderer. A serial killer. There are plenty of humans in the world who don't deserve to live."

"So you would play God?" He took a step toward me, but I didn't back down. "You would doom your soul to Hell for strength and immortality?"

"Not for strength and immortality," I told him. "For the freedom of knowing I would never have to be scared or helpless again."

We held each other's gazes, neither of us saying anything for a few seconds. Just because he was turned against his will didn't mean he could get me to change my mind. And if he wouldn't agree to turn me, then somehow, somewhere, I would find someone who would.

"Well, luckily for the both of us, you won't be turning into a vampire today." He bit his wrist again to open the wound and held it out to me. "But it won't be long until Camelia and her guards come after us again. This time, they'll have wormwood on them, so I won't be able to compel them. We need to be out of the Vale before they find us."

I reached for his arm, and fire rushed through my veins as my skin connected with his. His breathing slowed at my touch, and for a moment we stood there watching each other, neither of us saying a word. My eyes roamed to his lips, and I remembered what it had felt like to kiss them. Back in the alley, when I thought he was a human named Jake and that whatever attraction we felt together could be the start of something new.

It was the start of something new all right—just not in the way I expected.

"If you plan to survive what's coming, you need to do this," he said. "It'll give you the strength you need to get out of here."

"Temporarily," I reminded him.

"Yes." His eyes were hard—there was no changing his mind, at least right now. "Temporarily."

And so, I lowered my lips to his wrist and began to drink.

## 32

# JACEN

I SHUDDERED the moment her lips touched my skin.

Why did this girl—this stubborn, fiery human girl—have such a huge effect on me? Why was I risking so much to help her escape? Why couldn't I just hand her over to the guards and forget about her?

All I knew was that since meeting her, I'd felt more *alive* than I'd felt in the past year since being turned into a vampire. I didn't want to lose that feeling.

Therefore, I didn't want to lose her.

She continued to drink, pressing her mouth harder on my wrist and letting out a small groan as my blood passed her lips, as if she never wanted to stop.

But she'd taken more than a sufficient amount. If too much blood left my system, my strength would begin to weaken and I would need to feed again.

"Enough." I pried my wrist from her mouth, allowing my fingers to brush through her hair.

Her tongue lapped at the blood that remained on my skin, but I forced myself to pull away from her. Desire burned in her eyes as she looked at my wrist.

I used my other hand to tilt her chin up, forcing her gaze to meet mine.

She looked at me the same way she'd looked at my blood, and hot desire rushed through every inch of my body. I wanted to kiss her again. No—I wanted to do a hell of a lot more than kiss her. I wanted to lose myself in her entirely.

But did she still want me after knowing I'd lied to her?

We didn't have time right now to find out. Instead, I used my thumb to brush away the drops of blood that remained on her lips.

She sucked in a sharp breath as my skin touched hers, and reached for my other arm to steady herself.

Her touch felt colder than before—less human.

My blood must be working.

"How do you feel?" I asked, allowing my hand to drift back down to my side.

She still held onto my wrist, and I made no move to pull away. I told myself that that was because she might need to steady herself as the blood took affect, but really I knew—I just liked the feeling of her skin against mine.

"Strange," she said, her voice soft and breathy. "*Aware.*"

"The heightened senses of a vampire." I gazed down at her, slammed once more with the urge to kiss her.

"Yes." She looked around as if in a dream, although her hold on my arm tightened, making my heart pound faster.

It took every ounce of control to keep myself from pulling her to me and kissing her—especially knowing that this time, with my blood in her system making her stronger than the fragile human she normally was, I wouldn't have to hold back.

"I know it's night, but I can see as clearly as if it were day." She gazed around the mountains as if seeing them for the first time. "I can see the details of every leaf in every tree, and hear the soft chatter coming from the village, even though it's miles away. And I can hear something else—a river. It's soft, like it's calling to me..."

"My blood," I realized. "You're hearing the sound of my blood."

"You hear it too?" She refocused on me, looking startled. "In me?"

"I hear it in everyone."

"Is this what it feels like?" She swallowed. "To crave blood?"

"No," I told her. "When humans drink vampire blood, they don't experience the bloodlust like we do. In fact, right now, with my blood in your system, your blood doesn't call to me like a human's. I hear it, like I hear it in every supernatural creature, but I feel no urge to *drink* it. Until my blood leaves your system, that's what you should feel when you're around all types of blood—including human blood. You'll notice it, but you won't *crave* it."

"Oh." She frowned. "For a moment I thought it meant that if I were to turn into a vampire, I would be able to control my bloodlust."

I went silent, studying her. She looked paler than before—thanks to my blood—but her eyes still glimmered with hope and anticipation. She was full of so much *life.* Why was she so determined to have her mortality ripped away from her? To become a creature doomed to Hell?

"You don't need to become a vampire, Annika." I spoke slower this time, as if I could drill my opinion into her soul.

"It's easy for you to say that," she said. "You don't have to worry about always being the prey."

"Neither will you," I promised. "Once I free you from here, I'll make sure you're hidden in a place far away, where supernaturals will never find you—a place where you can live out your human life free of fear. Free from creatures like me."

"You know of such a place?" she asked.

"I've heard rumors," I told her, since it was true—I *had* heard talk of a location safe from supernaturals. An island accessible only to humans. "It's called the Sanctuary. Once we're out of the Vale, I'll find it and bring you there."

"And what about you?" she asked. "Will you go there too?"

"I can't." I chuckled. "In case you've forgotten, I'm a vampire. I would never be permitted inside."

Her eyes flashed with hurt, and I pulled my arm away from her touch. Because giving into the attraction between us would only result in pain and loss. So despite how much I wanted to pull her into my arms and kiss her again, I couldn't. I *wouldn't*.

I had to be strong for the both of us.

"Let's see if you're able to run fast enough to keep up with me," I said instead, changing the subject. "See that tree over there?" I pointed to the tallest tree at the end of the clearing.

"Yes," she said. "Every detail of it."

"Race me to it."

I took off, sensing her close behind. Ever since turning into a vampire, running felt more like flying. It was smooth and easy, leaving me exhilarated instead of breathless. I could run for miles on end and not get winded in the slightest.

Her hair—dark against the surrounding snow—flickered in my peripheral vision, and seconds before I arrived at the tree, she reached a hand out and beat me to it.

"Impressive," I told her. "Are you a runner?"

"I got a fair share of practice in the village," she said. "What about you? Were you a runner—before being turned?"

"A swimmer," I said quickly.

"I knew it!" She smiled. "You *are* that swimmer. The one who was going for the Olympics."

"I was," I said, my chest hollow at the reminder of who I used to be. "But I'm not that person anymore. Not since I was turned."

She lowered her eyes, saying nothing.

For once, I'd left the chatty human speechless.

Then she lifted her eyes back up, her strength returned. "I don't think you're a monster," she said softly. "I know you think you are, but you're not. If you were… you wouldn't be helping me right now."

"Maybe I'm only helping you to try to make up for every awful thing I've done this past year," I said, since that was easier than telling her why I was *really* helping her—because something about her made me unable to resist doing anything else.

"A true monster wouldn't care about repenting," she said confidently. "So... thank you, Jacen. This means a lot."

"Don't thank me yet," I said. "We're not even out of the Vale."

She glanced around the surrounding forest, worry crossing her face. "Are you *sure* the wolves won't attack us?" she asked.

"The wolves only attack humans," I told her. "With my blood in your system, they'll think we're two vampires. They'll have no reason to bother us."

"Okay." She took a deep breath, shaking away her worries. "I trust you."

"You shouldn't." I regretted the words the moment they were out of my mouth. Hadn't I been the one asking her to trust me back in the alley? Saying it had been instinctual, since once my blood was out of her system I would want to drink from her again. But I needed her to trust me now. I was her only hope. "I mean, you can trust me now. But in general, you should never trust a vampire. Always remember that."

"If you were going to hurt me, you would have already," she said. "I know you think you're a monster, but you're not."

"Tell that to me *after* we reach the Sanctuary," I told

her, since as much as I wanted to believe I wouldn't give into my bloodlust, who knew what would happen between now and then? I wouldn't feed on Annika, but I would need to feed eventually. Would she be so sure I wasn't a monster after witnessing such a thing?

"I will," she promised. "Now, which way out of the Vale?"

"Follow me."

I took off in a run, and she followed at my side.

# 33

# ANNIKA

THE BOUNDARY WAS CLEAR—LIKE a dome over the Vale—but it had a slight glimmer visible to those who knew it was there. I'd seen it as a human, but with vampire vision it was even more apparent. My instincts told me to slow as I approached it, but Jacen made no sign of slowing his pace, so I kept running. As I passed through the boundary, electricity passed over my skin—magical energy—and then it was gone.

I glanced behind, and sadness passed through my body. As much as I wanted to leave, there were people I didn't want to leave behind. Tanya, Norbert the bookshop manager, and all the others at the Tavern—these people had been the reasons why I'd survived my year in the Vale without giving up.

Now I was abandoning them.

But I wouldn't leave them forever. No—once Jacen and I found this Sanctuary, I would free the blood slaves of the Vale and bring them there. I wasn't sure how, but I would find a way. I owed it to them. I *had* to find a way.

Suddenly, Jacen thrust his arm in front of me, bringing me to a stop.

I looked to find out what made him pause, and that was when I saw them.

Wolves—an entire pack of them—surrounding us. Their teeth were drawn back, and they glared at us, looking ready to pounce.

"I thought you said the wolves wouldn't bother us?" I said to Jacen under my breath.

"I'll take care of this." He sounded sure of it, and he turned to face the wolf that was front and center—a big red one who appeared to be the leader of the pack.

The wolf's coloring reminded me of another wolf—one from nearly a year ago. But there were so many wolves in these woods. What were the chances I would run into the same one again?

"I am Prince Jacen of the Vale." He stood tall and proud, his tone conveying all the confidence of royalty. "My companion and I have done nothing to warrant this ambush. Let us pass."

The wolf snarled again, and then she shifted into human form. She was beautiful—tall, with bright red hair that flowed down to her waist. She wore a tight fitting, black body suit—it appeared that the suit shifted with her. I assumed it was created with magic. A necklace dangled from her neck, with a charm that resembled some sort of plant.

All of the other wolves remained in their animal form.

"That girl is no vampire," the redhead said calmly. "She's a human."

"Did you not see her running with me?" Jacen smirked, looking every bit an arrogant prince. "No human could run at that speed."

"She has ingested vampire blood. Most likely *your* blood," she said, and then she turned to me. "Did you not recognize me in my wolf form? I would think that night all those months ago would be one you would never forget..."

"You were the wolf who attacked me." I stood straighter, readying for trouble. "When I tried to escape the Vale."

"My name is Valerie, and I am the leader of this pack." She stuck her nose haughtily in the air. "When I attacked you all those months ago, I was perfectly within my rights. You were a human blood slave who'd crossed the boundary of the Vale. And I know enough about the ways of the vampires of the Vale to know that no blood slave of theirs has *ever* been approved to become a vampire. Queen Laila would never allow it."

"There are exceptions to every rule," Jacen said steadily. He still sounded confident, but he took a step closer to me, ready to protect me.

My stomach surged into my throat—hopefully it wouldn't come to a fight. I had no doubts that Jacen was a fantastic fighter, but two of us against this entire pack? The odds were not in our favor. Especially since my best skill was running—not fighting. And I knew better than to think that a bit of vampire blood would suddenly transform me into a trained warrior.

"True." Valerie held his gaze. "But a wolf's sense of smell is over ten times better than a vampire's. Vampires may not be able to smell the difference between a vampire and a human who has ingested vampire blood, but we can. Now—tell me. Why has a vampire prince given a human a taste of his blood and brought her out of the Vale?"

"The reason is irrelevant." Jacen glared at her and flashed his fangs. "We have an alliance. So unless you intend to go against a prince of the Vale—and therefore go against the entire *kingdom*—you will let us pass. Now."

"The alliance is less and less relevant to us as of late," she said with a wave of her hand. "Centuries ago, vampires stole a piece of our land—the area you now call the Vale. The treaty stated that to avoid a war between the species, we would keep the Vale safe from intruders as long as the vampires let us live in peace and didn't expand further into our territory. At the time, we were outnumbered and had no choice but to agree. If we hadn't agreed, we would have been slaughtered. However, we're growing in numbers faster than you can imagine. And you've transformed the land you stole from us into a kingdom far more bountiful than we could have ever imagined."

"Queen Laila created the kingdom of the Vale from the ground up," Jacen said. "It *never* would have become what it is now if it had been left in your hands."

"Maybe not." Valerie shrugged. "But while the vampires of the Vale may have forgotten who that land originally belonged to, I assure you, we have not."

"What are you saying?" Jacen bristled. "You're going to fight for it back?"

"You're free to make any assumptions you want." She smiled sweetly. "Not that it matters... since once we're finished with you, there will be nothing left for anyone to find."

# 34

## JACEN

I HELD an arm out in front of Annika, protecting her. If only I'd known that wolves could smell when a human had ingested vampire blood… I tried to think of what else I could have done, but came up blank. An older vampire would have known. But I had truly thought this plan would work. I thought I was saving Annika.

Turned out I was only bringing her from being hunted by vampires to being hunted by wolves.

There had to be a way out of this mess. It was well known that the wolves protected themselves against our compulsion with wormwood, which was apparent by the wormwood charm around Valerie's neck. And the strength of wolves matched that of vampires, so with eight of them against the two of us, fighting would be too risky. Especially because my training was limited to what I'd learned this past year, and Annika had no training at all.

I glanced around the woods, sizing up my surroundings to figure out my next move.

Then Valerie shifted back into wolf form.

Before she had a chance to pounce, I grabbed Annika's arm and jumped. Annika must have had a similar idea, because the two of us landed firmly on a branch of a tree at least ten feet from the ground.

Valerie landed face first in the snow.

She stood up and shook the snow off her fur, and the other wolves paced around the base of the tree. All of them growled up at us.

"I thought you said the wolves wouldn't attack us," Annika said through gritted teeth.

I just ripped a branch off the tree, aimed it down at one of the wolves, and threw.

It impaled the wolf straight through its back, pinning it to the ground. Blood splattered in the snow underneath of it. The wolf dropped its head and went still.

"One down," I growled, snapping another branch off the tree. "Seven to go."

I aimed this one at Valerie, but she rolled out of the way, the branch missing her by a few inches.

Annika snapped another branch off the tree, preparing to aim.

"We have a limited number of branches here before we'll have to jump to the next tree and start again," I warned her. "How's your aim?"

"Let's see." She propelled the branch down, getting one of the other wolves—a gray one—in his shoulder.

The wolf whimpered, blood dripping onto the snow, but the blow wasn't fatal.

"Nice." I nodded, impressed that she'd managed to hit a wolf at all. "Where'd you learn how to aim like that?"

"Darts." She shrugged. "We play a lot at the Tavern."

Valerie grabbed the branch out of the gray wolf's side with her teeth, and the bleeding slowed.

The wolf took a few heavy breaths, and then it stood on its hind legs, balancing its front paws on tree trunk and growling.

Annika's face fell. "The wolf's healing," she realized.

"You need to get them in the heart," I told her. "That shot would have killed a regular wolf—it would have bled out—but these are shifters. They have healing abilities similar to vampires."

The gray wolf was being reckless—standing that way exposed its chest.

In a flash, I broke off another branch and threw it down, impaling the wolf straight through its heart.

It fell backward, the thrust of the throw shooting it

to the ground. The wolf landed on its back. Its eyes were blank, and the branch stuck up toward the sky.

One of the other wolves—a snowy white one—let out a long howl and ran toward the gray wolf, poking him with her nose. She howled again and again, the pain-filled cries echoing through the forest.

I could only guess that the fallen wolf had been her mate.

"We didn't come here to fight," I yelled down to them, loud enough to be heard over the howls. "No one else has to die today. Just let us pass."

Valerie shifted back into human form and sped over to the corpse of the gray wolf, yanking the branch out of its chest. "You've killed two of my pack." She snarled. "And you're going to pay." She pulled her arm back, red hair flying in the wind as she heaved the branch up toward Annika.

I shielded the human girl with my body and moved us both to the side, but we didn't have much room to move in the tree. Pain shot through my body as the branch entered my back near my right shoulder. I sucked in a deep breath, stopping myself from crying out.

Vampires might be able to heal, but every injury hurt us just as much as it would a human. More so, because our senses were heightened.

Annika held onto both of my arms, steadying me to

stop me from falling. "You risked your life to save me," she realized, staring up at me in wonder. "If you hadn't done that…"

"The branch would have gone straight through your heart." I reached behind myself and yanked out the branch, breathing steadily as I felt the skin knit together. The injury—and the energy it took to heal it—would cost me. I would have to feed sooner than intended.

But I couldn't worry about that now. Right now, my *only* worry was defeating the wolves.

I turned around as another branch soared toward us, but I threw my arm out, catching it mid-air. I shot it back down toward Valerie at the same time as she threw another branch up at us.

I reached for Annika's hand, trying to anticipate the path of the branch so we could both avoid it.

But both branches came to a sudden stop mid-air. They floated there, as if someone had pressed pause, and I held my breath as I stared at them.

I only knew of one creature capable of performing such a feat.

A witch.

Camelia had found us.

# 35

## ANNIKA

THE FLOATING BRANCHES FLEW UP, over the treetops, and out into the depths of the forest.

Suddenly the tree tilted, and I gripped Jacen's hand as the tree tipped slowly to the side until we couldn't hold our balance any more. We both rolled out of the branches, the snow cushioning our fall.

The wolves turned away from the Vale and ran.

Once we stopped rolling, I saw a cluster of boots in front of us.

"Well, well, well," a familiar voice said from above. "If it isn't the blood slave I was looking for."

I stood up, brushing the snow off myself and glaring at her. She was backed by what looked to be twenty vampire guards. In seconds, they formed a circle around us.

"Camelia," I said her name steadily, holding my gaze with hers. With Jacen's blood in my system, I felt stronger than ever. Yes, vampire guards surrounded us, and yes, our odds were now *worse* than they'd been when we were only against the wolves, but at least I was more powerful than I would have been as a human.

Jacen reached for my hand again and held it tightly, as if trying to tell me not to say anything more.

Camelia looked down at our clasped hands and raised an eyebrow. "Daniel informed me about the... state he and his men discovered the two of you in when they went to find the girl at the Tavern," she said, her voice so eerily calm that it raised the hairs on my arms. "And I see you've given her a taste of your blood. You do know the long term effects of that, do you not?"

Jacen just stared at her, his gaze so dark and hollow that I wondered if he was planning on demolishing her and the guards in a single swoop.

"What's so special about this blood slave?" Camelia continued, smiling as if his murderous expression didn't bother her in the slightest. "Why has a vampire prince gone so out of his way to attempt to free her from the Vale?"

"Why did you send the guards to take her?" Jacen tightened his grip around my hand, his voice cold. "With explicit instructions not to harm her?"

"You're always looking for trouble, aren't you?"

Camelia laughed, the sound high and melodic, like bells. "I shouldn't have expected anything less. First that murder spree you went on in the village last year, and now this."

I gasped, pulling my hand out of his. "Murder spree?" I repeated, but as his face fell, it all made sense. All of the information I'd known, but hadn't put together until now.

Jacen had been turned into a vampire soon before I'd been brought to the Vale. I, and many others who'd been kidnapped around that time, had been needed because a freshly turned vampire had lost control of his bloodlust and rampaged the village. It had been a bloodbath. Mike's parents had both been killed. Nearly *everyone* who lived in the Vale knew someone who'd been killed.

If those murders had never happened, the vampires wouldn't have needed to recruit so many humans last year. They wouldn't have kidnapped me. They wouldn't have murdered my family.

The vampire who had lost control was responsible for so many lives lost.

But that vampire had been caught and executed.

At least, that was what I'd been told.

"He never told you?" Camelia smirked, speaking to me since the first time she found us. "And here I thought the two of you were close."

"It was you." I looked to Jacen, wanting to hear it from him—not from her. "You killed all those people in the village last year."

"I warned you I was dangerous," he said darkly. "I've built up my strength so I can now control the bloodlust, but when I first turned... it consumed me. That night, I didn't even know what I'd done until afterward."

I backed away, unable to look at him. Because yes, I knew vampires struggled with bloodlust. I knew they'd all killed.

But most of them didn't go on mass murder sprees through an entire village.

The worst part was that I'd trusted him. I was going to let him help me escape.

Was he even trying to help me at all? Or was this some elaborate plan concocted from the first night he'd met me? He never *did* explain why he'd asked me to dance that night instead of any of the other humans in the town square. And for unknown reasons, Camelia clearly wanted me in the palace.

I'd been a pawn this entire time.

As a human, I would *always* be a pawn in the supernaturals' game.

"The two of you were working together this whole time, weren't you?" I voiced my hypothesis out loud.

"No." Jacen reached for my hand, but with his blood

in my system I was just as fast as he was, and I pulled away.

"This is getting better by the second." Camelia looked back and forth between the two of us, that smug smile still on her face. "You didn't *actually* think a vampire prince would care about a human blood slave —at least as anything more than a play toy. Or did you?"

I wanted to say that yes, Jacen cared about helping me escape. But did he? After all, he hated that he'd been turned into a vampire against his will—he'd told me that much, and I believed him. He also knew that Camelia wanted me, for reasons unknown to both of us.

What better way to anger the leaders of the Vale than to steal away something they wanted?

"Don't listen to her," Jacen said. "She's lying."

"As if you're any better?" I snapped. "You lied to me from the moment you met me. You made me believe you were human."

His eyes flashed with hurt, and for a moment I felt guilty. But only for a moment. Because I owed none of them anything. As long as I was human, I was worse than trash to *all* of the supernaturals in and around the Vale. None of them could be trusted.

"As much as I'm enjoying watching your pathetic drama, this game has gone far enough," Camelia interrupted. "Annika needs to come with me to the palace. Now."

I looked around, but the vampire guards surrounded us. Escape was impossible. Still, I had to try. After all, I'd always been quick. Nimble. With my temporary vampire strength, perhaps I stood a chance.

These woods were huge. All I needed was to get far enough away that they would lose my trail.

It was risky. But better to take the risk than be brought back to the palace for unknown reasons that would likely result in my death.

So I leaped into the air, aiming for the branch of the nearest tree. But right before reaching the tree, I smacked into an invisible wall and crashed back onto the snow.

Camelia must have cast some sort of barrier around us. Similar to the boundaries around the Vale, but keeping us *in* instead of keeping others out.

My head pounded, and I blinked a few times to get the stars out of my vision. When I finally steadied myself enough to look up, I saw Jacen fighting with five of the guards. One of the guards was already lying in the snow beside him, his neck twisted in an unnatural position. Jacen snapped another guard's neck, and he went down beside his comrade.

They weren't dead—they would heal—but not for a few hours.

I forced myself back up, ready to help him fight. I could come up from behind and snap another guard's neck. They would never see it coming.

But before I could start to run, something pricked the back of my neck—a needle.

I opened my mouth to warn Jacen, but the world spun around me, and everything went dark.

# 36

# ANNIKA

I WOKE UP SHIVERING. The floor was hard and rough, uneven spots jamming into various places in my body. Everything hurt—my legs, my arms, and mainly my head. My stomach, too.

I'd only been hungover once—New Year's Day sophomore year, when a group of us had stayed over one of my friends houses whose parents were away. We'd all had *way* too much champagne while celebrating New Year's Eve, and had woken up the next morning feeling like crap.

This felt similar, except multiplied by a hundred.

I lay there, unable to find the energy to open my eyes, and all my recent memories flooded back to me.

Jacen coming to see me at the Tavern, kissing him in the alley, the vampire guards coming for me, Jacen revealing he was a vampire prince, the two of us running away, my drinking his blood, escaping the Vale, confronting the wolves, and finally, the fight with Camelia and the vampire guards.

They'd injected me with something.

What had they given me? How long had I been out?

And what had happened to Jacen?

I groaned and rolled over in the dirt. I needed to open my eyes and figure out where I was, but I had a dreadful feeling that I wasn't going to like what I would find.

"I expect you're feeling like Hell," a familiar voice said—Camelia.

Her irritating voice felt like pinpricks in my brain.

I doubled over and retched, heaving out everything I'd eaten in the past day. The smell filled my nose, making me retch again, until my stomach was empty. The mess was all over the dirt floor beside me—bile mixed with blood.

I rolled over to my other side, not wanting to look at it.

There were bars in front of me—this dirt-floored room must be a prison. And sitting beyond the bars, on a small beach chair sipping a margarita, was Camelia.

"You *look* like Hell, too," she said with that irritating smirk. "In case you were wondering."

"What did you give me?" I croaked, forcing myself to

sit up and lean against the stone wall. I reached behind my neck to where the needle had entered—the area was puffy and sore.

"Just a sedative." She shrugged. "But that's not why you feel like crap."

"Enlighten me, then." I glared at her, having a feeling from the way she smiled in return that she couldn't *wait* to do so.

"You drank Jacen's blood," she said. "Which gave you the abilities of a vampire for a day. But you didn't think doing so would come without consequences, did you?"

He'd never told me about any consequences. But I remained silent, not wanting *her* to know that.

"You did, didn't you?" She laughed. "You humans are so naive. Would you like to hear what the consequences are?"

I stared at her, waiting. Then, realizing she wasn't going to continue without my asking, I forced out a strained yes.

"I thought so," she said with a smile. "The vampire blood temporarily gives you strength, but it takes a *huge* toll on your body. You won't feel normal for a week, at best. But there are ways to speed up the recovery process…" She took a sip of her margarita and watched me, clearly baiting me again.

I said nothing. I wasn't going to give into her silly games.

But I also could barely move. My head spun, my mouth tasted like sandpaper, and my muscles felt like they'd been torn to shreds. If there was a way to feel better, I wanted to know.

"What ways?" I finally gave in.

"Most usually jump for more vampire blood." She smiled. "That would do the trick instantly. But there's also an herbal remedy I can whip up—it'll make that hangover disappear in hours instead of a week."

"And why do I have a feeling you *won't* be supplying me with either one of those?" I asked.

"I won't be, but not for the reasons you might think." She tilted her head and pulled her hair over her shoulders, somehow managing to look regal despite sitting in a beach chair in a dungeon. "Firstly, you've done nothing to deserve the herbal remedy. And as for the vampire blood… the human body isn't meant to have power like that. It feels fun at first—exhilarating. Addicting. But over time, it would wear your poor, weak body down, fast-forwarding the aging process until killing you completely. And neither of us want that to happen to you, now do we?"

I clenched my hands into fists, my nails digging into my palms. Why hadn't Jacen told me about any of that? He'd just given me his blood recklessly, and I'd taken it.

Once more, I cursed myself for trusting a vampire. It was yet another reminder that as long as I was human, I would be a pawn in a game ruled by supernaturals.

"Where am I?" I asked, wanting to change the subject. I had a good idea about where I was, but I needed to hear it officially.

"The dungeons of the palace, of course," she answered. "But don't worry—you're not a prisoner. We simply needed to keep you somewhere you couldn't escape from until the vampire blood left your system."

"If I'm not a prisoner, then why am I behind bars?"

"Because if you don't agree to what I ask, then you *will* be a prisoner," she said firmly. "I thought it would be best to give you a taste of what your short future would hold if you decline my offer."

I looked around the small cell. It was dank and dingy, without even a place to sit. The only item inside of it was a small pot—likely the equivalent of a toilet. But the strangest thing about the dungeon was how quiet it was.

"Are there any others here?" I asked. "Or am I the only one?"

"There are others," Camelia answered. "But I've cast a sound barrier around us to keep our conversation private. After all, I have an important proposition for you, and I don't want anyone listening in."

"The same proposition that killed Mike?" I glared at

her. She opened her mouth to speak, but I continued before she could. "Don't tell me he's alive. The vampire guards already told me otherwise."

She sat back, apparently taken by surprise that I knew about Mike's fate. But the shock disappeared from her face a second later, her expression returning to its mask of calm.

"I never wanted Mike to die." She looked down as she spoke—almost as if she were grieving—and then refocused on me. "Only a human can accomplish the task I need done, and he was so strong—with the way he defeated that wolf—that I felt sure he could succeed. But his death wasn't in vain."

"No?" I raised an eyebrow, raking my nails through the dirt floor to keep from breaking at the reminder that I would never see my friend again.

"I sent him to obtain an extremely valuable object," she said. "He didn't succeed, but he got something nearly as important—a rare seeing crystal that told me *exactly* who could obtain the object in question. Only a powerful witch can use the crystal—it took even myself a few weeks to master—but you can only imagine my surprise when the crystal showed me an image of you."

"Me?" I asked in disbelief. "Why would it show me?"

"Trust me, I have as little of an idea as you," she said. "I see nothing special about you—a dirty human blood slave. But alas, it *did* show you. And the crystal doesn't lie. You are the human destined to retrieve the sapphire ring that contains the powerful witch Geneva."

And from there, she told me exactly what she wanted me to do.

# 37

# ANNIKA

"So," Camelia said once she'd finished explaining the task. "What do you say?"

I thought about her offer, balancing my options. Apparently, I was the only human in the entire world who could enter this Crystal Cavern and retrieve the sapphire ring that imprisoned the most powerful witch in the world, Geneva.

But why me?

It made no sense.

On the other hand, refusal would mean rotting away in this prison until the day I died. And Camelia *needed* me. Which meant I had the upper hand. And while I hated her for what she let happen to Mike, I knew that Mike wouldn't want me to let this opportunity go to waste. He would want me to use it to free myself—to escape the Vale once and for all, and to never be at the mercy of the vampires again.

"I'll do as you ask," I finally said. "But only for a cost."

"Your reward is that you won't be locked in this prison." She balked. "What more could you possibly want?"

"I want to be turned into a vampire."

Her eyes flashed with surprise, and she set her nearly finished margarita down in the cup holder. "Why on Earth would you want that?" she asked. "I thought the humans here hated the vampires."

"I don't hate them nearly as much as I hate being at their mercy," I told her.

"A blood slave has *never* been turned in the history of the Vale," she said. "You're unfit for the transformation."

"Do you mean that I wouldn't survive the transformation because I've given blood to the vampires?" I asked. "Because if what you say is true and a blood slave has never been turned into a vampire, I don't see how you could possibly know if that's a fact or not."

"You're unfit because you're tainted," she said simply. "You're not worthy."

"So it's merely a prejudice," I concluded. "And apparently according to this seeing crystal, I'm worthy enough to fetch this sapphire ring—worthier than any other human in the world. So if you need me as much as you claim, you'll grant my request."

She eyed me up for a few seconds, thinking. "Fine," she eventually said. "If you succeed in bringing me Geneva's sapphire ring, I'll speak to Queen Laila on your behalf and recommend that you become a vampire." She stood up and brushed herself off, as if she considered the conversation done.

"Wait," I called out, and she turned around, glaring at me once more. "While I appreciate your promise, your word is not enough," I said, enjoying how her expression hardened at my words. "I want us to make a blood oath."

"Why am I not surprised," Camelia said bitterly. "It took a blood oath to convince Mike, too."

"Because Mike was smart." My heart panged at the memory of my friend—at the reminder that I would never see him again. "He took me under his wing after I was brought here. And one thing he drilled into my mind was this—never trust the word of a supernatural, unless they've made a blood oath."

"Very well." Camelia sighed, pulled a knife out of her boot, and slit her palm. "Now, give me your hand."

"Give me your knife," I demanded instead.

She raised an eyebrow. "I'm not giving you the knife," she said. "Give me your hand. Unless you don't wish to continue?"

"Fine." I sighed and held my hand out, since after all, I was merely testing her. I wasn't naive enough to think the knife would help me escape my current situation.

She made a similar incision on my palm, and I bit the inside of my cheek to stop myself from grunting from the pain. Once done, she wiped the knife clean, shoved it back inside her boot, and clasped her hand with mine.

"I promise that if you give me Geneva's sapphire ring, I'll tell Queen Laila of your feat and will do everything in my power to convince her to turn you into a vampire," she said. "Do you swear to agree to this blood oath?"

"That's not enough," I told her. "I want you to promise that you *will* have me turned into a vampire."

"As I am not a vampire myself, it's not in my power to make such a promise," she said. "But I *have* sworn my best effort to speak on your behalf, and as Queen Laila respects my opinions, she will likely listen." She leaned closer, her eyes narrowing. "This is the best promise you can possibly hope for, girl. You're closer to the chance of becoming a vampire than any blood slave in history. So do you accept, or not?"

"I accept," I said, and the moment I spoke the words, warm energy rushed through my body, starting at the place where my hand met Camelia's. A golden aura glowed around both of our hands, growing hotter and hotter, as if burning the oath into our souls.

The glow eventually died down, and Camelia pulled her hand out of mine.

I examined my palm—the cut was gone.

"It is done," Camelia confirmed. "We'll leave for the mountain at dawn. In the meantime, I'll brew the herbal remedy and will bring it down for you when it's ready. You'll need your energy for what's to come.

The chair and margarita glass vanished with a snap of her fingers, and then she turned around, leaving me alone in the dungeon.

## 38

## JACEN

I AWOKE in my bed to find Laila and multiple guards looking down on me, surrounding me.

"Where is she?" I shot up, grabbed Laila by the neck, and pinned her to the wall. "Where's Annika?"

The guards pulled me off of her, and she waved them away, as if their help wasn't necessary.

"I do not know where the girl is," Laila said calmly. "Camelia was the one who wanted her—not I."

"Don't act like you have no idea why," I told her. "Camelia answers to you. If Camelia wanted Annika, you know the reason."

"I think it's best you speak to Camelia about that." Laila smiled. "How are you feeling, by the way? The guards had to inject you with a double dose of wormwood to knock you out. Quite impressive, if you ask me —a testament to your strength."

I rubbed the back of my arm—the spot they'd jabbed me with the needle. It had happened soon after they'd knocked out Annika. I'd been fighting the guards, and then I'd seen one of them jab a needle in her neck. It had only taken that one moment—that short distraction—for one of the guards to catch me unaware.

"I'm going to find Camelia," I declared, standing up and heading for the door. Once I found Camelia, I would find Annika. And once I found Annika…

Well, I wasn't sure *what* I would do once I found her. For now, I just needed to know she was alive.

"Wait." Laila held out a hand, and the guards rushed to the doors, blocking my path. "After your first shot of wormwood, you were awake but in a state of delirium. The guards reported you said something curious…"

"And what was that?" I asked, because the faster I gave into her little mind games, the faster I would be free to find Annika.

"You said that Annika would be safe because she was wearing wormwood."

"No I didn't," I said instantly, hating my half unconscious self for revealing such a thing. I didn't even remember it—the wormwood they'd injected me with must have made me truly delirious.

"You did," she continued. "So we checked the girl for any trace of wormwood. We found none."

I stared at her, shocked. How could that be? Annika couldn't be compelled—she *had* to have been wearing wormwood. There was no other explanation for her resistance to my magic.

But I stood straighter, composing myself. I wasn't sure how it was possible for a human to be immune to compulsion, but if it were, bringing it to light would put Annika under more scrutiny than before. They might even kill her.

If the vampires hated one thing above anything else, it was a threat to their power.

"I have no idea why I would have said that," I said instead, trying to act nonchalant. "Clearly I was delirious."

"Clearly," Laila agreed, although she didn't look convinced. "Why is this human so important to you, anyway?" she asked. "Who is she to you?"

"She's no one," I said, since that *should* have been the truth. All she'd been at first was a pretty girl I'd noticed at the village festival. But somehow, with everything that had happened between us in such a short amount of time, she'd become more than that. I'd come to care about her.

More than that—I had a *responsibility* to her. Because

if I hadn't noticed her that night, I had a feeling that none of this would have happened.

She was in danger from the vampires because of me. I'd created this mess. Therefore, I had to be the one to make sure she was safe.

"Good," Camelia said, throwing open my doors and bursting into the room. "If she's no one to you, then you won't care that she's dead."

# 39

# CAMELIA

I KNEW Jacen was lying the moment he said he didn't care about the human girl, but the way his face dropped when I announced her death only further affirmed it.

He cared about her.

Which was exactly why I had to make sure he thought he had no chance of ever seeing her again.

"The girl was a thief." I made my way to the center of the room, taking notice of the way all eyes were on me. "Why do you think the guards were sent to bring her to the dungeons in the first place?"

"She wasn't a thief," he said. "You don't even know her."

"And you do?" I raised an eyebrow. "She stole from the vampires. She stole food that wasn't permitted for humans—candies, cheese, meats—and gave them to her co-workers at the Tavern."

"A human stole from the vampires?" Jacen balked. "Impossible."

"If you don't believe me, you can ask the workers at the Tavern yourself," I continued. "It didn't take long for us to get them to turn her in. The blood slaves have no loyalty—the sooner you learn that, the better. They would do anything to save themselves and their families, even if it means turning in a friend. She's dead," I repeated, wanting to rub it in further. "And now she'll never be able to steal from the vampires again."

"I don't believe you." He narrowed his eyes and rushed at me, but the guards stopped him before he could get close. He fought their hold, but even a vampire prince wasn't strong enough to free himself from five guards—especially when his emotions were getting the best of him. "Show her to me."

I smiled, because of course I'd already planned for this.

"Bring the body here," I told Daniel. "It's in cell thirty-one."

Daniel whizzed out of the room, and Jacen stared at me, his eyes dark.

"If you killed her..." he started, clenching his fists to his sides.

"Then what?" I asked. "I did nothing out of line. The

girl stole from vampires and has been punished for her crimes. She'll be an example to the blood slaves about what happens when our rules are broken. They need a good example every now and then to make sure they remember their place."

No one spoke as we waited for Daniel to return. And with his vampire speed, it didn't take long for him to come back, hauling Annika's body behind him and dropping it on the ground.

Her skin was paler than ever, her blood drained dry. Not a drop of it had been left behind.

I crossed my arms and stared at my work, proud of myself for flawlessly putting this into play. Because after hearing of Annika and Jacen's escape from the guards, I'd gone to the Tavern myself to investigate. There, I'd met a girl who claimed to be one of Annika's closest friends—Tanya, I believe was her name—and had her brought to the dungeons for questioning. She had no memories of Jacen—she'd either never met him or he'd compelled her to forget him—but she *did* confess about Annika's stealing vampire food and sharing it with the humans who worked at that dingy human bar.

I'd originally intended to release her back into the village to show her some gratitude for coming clean about her friend. But then I'd seen the way Jacen and Annika had looked at each other in the mountains. He cared about the mousey human blood slave. I didn't understand *why,* but he wasn't going to stop fighting for her no matter what.

Unless he thought she was dead.

So, while Annika had been passed out in her cell, I'd taken a strand of her hair. Transformation potions were my specialty, so it hadn't taken long to brew. And of course, getting Tanya to drink it had been easy. The girl had barely been given any food or drink since arriving in the dungeons, and she'd downed the first thing placed in front of her—the potion.

Her body had transformed into Annika's in minutes.

All I'd needed to do from there was call a vampire guard into the cell and instruct him to drain her dry. The guards were rarely given blood straight from the vein—that was a luxury typically reserved for the royals and nobles—so he'd been more than happy to oblige.

All of this had been done before Annika had awoken from her sedative.

I'd cast a spell around her cell to make it appear empty, and to block all sound coming in and out of it. No one knew she was there. No one except me, of course. And she wouldn't be there for long, since we were leaving for the Crystal Cavern at dawn.

As for that pesky blood oath she'd insisted upon making... she wouldn't be in my hair for much longer if she ended up dead. Which was exactly what I planned on having happen—after she brought me Geneva's sapphire ring and was turned into a vampire.

Nothing in our oath prevented me from killing her *after* she was turned.

Jacen stared at the body, saying nothing.

I watched him curiously. I *thought* he'd cared about the girl, but he was betraying no emotion. As if she meant nothing to him.

"Well?" I crossed my arms, focused only on him. "Do you believe me now?"

His eyes flicked up to meet mine, and they were so empty that I nearly took a step back. For the first time since he'd turned, I saw in him the true makings of a vampire prince.

The vampire prince who would someday be mine.

"Take her away," he said, his voice hard and strong.

No one moved a muscle. The guards glanced around, appearing as taken aback by his reaction as I felt.

"Did you not hear me?" His eyes darkened, and he glared at the guards. "I am your prince—you answer to me. And I am commanding you to take her away!"

The body was out of the room in seconds.

"Have her strung up in the village square for the next twelve hours," I told the guards who remained. "As an example to everyone there about what happens to those who break our rules. Once the twelve hours are up, feed her to the wolves."

I couldn't help smiling at how perfectly this had panned out. The transformation spell would only last for three days—then the corpse would revert back to its true appearance—but the wolves would ensure that nothing remained.

No one would ever know the truth.

"This amuses you," Jacen observed, his gaze still locked on mine.

"And it seems to not affect you," I countered.

"Like you said, the girl was only a blood slave." His voice was so cold that it brought goosebumps to my arms. "She was pretty, but my attraction to her was only physical. After getting bored with her—which I'm sure wouldn't have taken long—I likely would have drained her dry myself."

I raised an eyebrow. "So why go to the trouble to help her escape?" I asked.

"It seemed like an amusing challenge." He shrugged. "An adventure. Can you blame me, after being confined in this palace for nearly a year? I needed a little fun."

"I suppose not," I said, matching his indifference. I wasn't sure if I believed him or not, but I would play this game with him—for now. "So, let's all be glad that justice has been served. We cannot have rebels in our midst. I helped you, Jacen. Not just you, but all the vampires in the kingdom. I hope you don't forget it when it's time for you to choose a bride."

"Trust me, I won't," he said, and then he turned to face Laila.

The vampire queen stood near the window, where she'd been watching this entire scene play out. If any of it fazed her, she didn't let it show.

"Put out a call for the eligible princesses from the six kingdoms to come to the palace at once," he told her. "I will meet them, and we will enact your idea of creating a show of the whole event. Because soon, I will choose one of them to join my side as a future princess of the Vale."

# 40

# ANNIKA

THE DUNGEONS WERE SO dark and empty that I had no sense of time.

After Camelia had given me the potion to cure my vampire blood hangover, I'd tried calling out to the humans in the other cells. No one answered. I was either alone, or still trapped within the sound barrier she'd casted earlier.

I'd searched the cell for an escape, but found none. I hadn't thought I would. No human had ever escaped the dungeons. Once they were brought here, they were never heard from again.

There was no way out on my own. So I shivered and lay on the floor, reminding myself of the blood oath. While it might feel like it, my situation was far from hopeless. I wasn't just another human who'd been brought here to be fine dining for a royal vampire.

For some reason, Camelia's special seeing crystal believed *I* was destined to find this sapphire ring she desired so badly. And once I brought her the ring, I would get what I'd wanted for months—I would become a vampire. I could leave the Vale and fend for myself in the world of supernaturals. I would no longer be weak. I would no longer be hunted.

I wasn't sure where I would go after becoming a vampire, but at least I would be free. And hopefully, wherever I went, Jacen would come with me. We hadn't known each other for long, but there was a connection between us—I felt it, and I knew he felt it too. He wouldn't have tried to help me escape if he hadn't. He wouldn't have fought the vampire guards after Camelia had found us in the woods. I believed him that he'd changed since going on that murderous rampage one year ago.

However, he was a vampire prince destined to help rule this kingdom. He couldn't just up and leave.

Then again, maybe staying in the Vale as a vampire wouldn't be the worst thing in the world, especially with the ears of the prince. Perhaps, with Jacen's help, the two of us could change the way the entire kingdom was run. We could petition Queen Laila to stop kidnapping humans, give them actual rights… and give them a choice if they wanted to stay or leave.

But I was getting ahead of myself. I needed to take this one step at a time.

The first step was completing Camelia's task and getting that sapphire ring.

Finally, after what felt like forever, Camelia arrived at my cell. She wore all black—as always—the only color on her outfit was the green pendant she wore around her neck.

"It's dawn," she informed me. "How are you feeling?"

"Better," I told her, since it was true. The potion she'd given me hadn't just cured my hangover—it made me feel like I'd just eaten a full meal, too.

"Good." She lowered herself so she was level with me, reached for my arm through the bars, and suddenly, the world vanished around me.

# 41

## ANNIKA

In an instant, we were standing on a snow-covered mountain—and my entire body felt like it had been turned inside out.

Camelia let go of my arm and I fell to the ground.

The world spun around me, and I took a few deep breaths, holding onto the ground to steady myself. There were no trees around us, and the air felt so thin that I had to focus on making sure I had enough of it to breathe.

"What..." I started, looking up at her in shock. "What did you just do? Where are we?"

"We're at the peak of the mountain that leads to the Crystal Cavern," she told me. "The entrance is right behind you. I teleported us here."

"*Teleported?*" I repeated, turning around to see this

entrance she spoke of. Sure enough, there was a slim opening in the rocks, leading into what appeared to be pitch-black darkness.

"The act of transporting across a distance instantaneously," she said simply.

"I know what the word means," I snapped, standing up and brushing the snow off my jeans. "I just didn't know it was possible."

"It takes a significant amount of magic," she said. "Especially when teleporting someone with me. So I only do it when necessary."

"You didn't teleport with Mike." I shivered, my wet jeans feeling like ice on my skin. I wrapped my arms around myself, trying to warm up, but it didn't do much to help. "You brought him on your golf cart."

Camelia waved her hand, and my jeans were dry. She also must have created some kind of warmth bubble around us, because the temperature rose from hypothermia inducing to somewhat tolerable. "I dropped him off at the base of the mountain," she said. "Teleporting him wasn't necessary."

"And it was with me?" I asked.

"Yes." She narrowed her eyes, her voice like ice.

"I suppose you're not going to tell me why?"

"No." She smiled and pulled something out of her bag—a flashlight. "Take this. You're going to need it."

I took it from her and pressed the button to make sure it worked.

It did.

"The batteries are fresh," she said. "It'll have more than enough juice to light your way through the cavern."

"Thank you." I gripped the flashlight, gazing back at the entrance to the cave.

"Wait to thank me until you have that ring," she said. "And remember—touch nothing in the cavern other than the ring."

"Why?" I quickly shifted my focus back to her. "What will happen if I do?"

"The cavern is full of dangerous items." She lowered her voice, as if afraid someone would overhear. "They're items of dark magic. There are reasons they're locked in there. For example, the seeing crystal. It has such strong powers that if someone other than a witch touches it, it scorches them to death. Like what happened to your friend Mike."

I shuddered at the image that flashed through my mind.

"It wasn't pretty." She nodded, as if to rub it in.

"And the sapphire ring?" I asked. "Why am I able to retrieve it and no one else?"

"I have no idea." Camelia scowled. "The seeing crystal wouldn't reveal that information. But make sure that once you find the ring, you don't touch the gem. Touch only the setting."

"What happens if I touch the gem?" I asked.

"So many questions." Camelia rolled her eyes. "Don't you realize that everything I'm telling you is for your own safety?"

"I'm just curious," I told her. "Sorry."

She watched me for a few seconds, as if contemplating how much to reveal. "Touching the gem will release great magic," she said with a huff. "You can't risk touching it without a witch nearby to protect you."

"I assume you're referring to yourself?" I asked.

"Who else?" She straightened her shoulders. "We made a blood oath—I'm bound by magic to ensure you survive this mission, so that I can see through your transformation into vampire. If I break the oath, my blood will turn to poison and I'll die. We're on the same side. I'm not sure what else I can do to prove it."

I pressed my lips together, saying nothing. After all, she had a point. Camelia might have inadvertently gotten Mike killed—and I would never forget it—but I needed to stop thinking of her as the enemy.

"You're right." I turned to face the cave, taking another deep breath to calm my nerves and readying the flashlight.

"Of course I am," she said. "Now—go. And don't come back out until you have that ring."

## 42

# ANNIKA

I ENTERED THE CAVE, using the flashlight to guide my way. The interior looked exactly like I'd imagined—empty, with rock walls and a dirt ceiling. It smelled wet and musty, and the walls shined under the light. But the strangest thing was the temperature. The mountain had been cold—as expected in the Canadian Rockies. The inside of the cave was the perfect temperature. So perfect, in fact, that I had to remove my outer layers.

I turned a corner, stopping at the sight ahead—winding steps that seemed to go down forever. They were made out of rock, appearing to be *part* of the cave. There was also no railing. Someone could easily lose their balance and fall straight down the center. I doubted I would lose my balance—my gymnast skills would certainly come in handy—but if I needed to use these stairs, I would still be extra careful.

I peered over them and shined my flashlight down, unable to see to the bottom. Curious, I picked up a nearby pebble and threw it down the center of the stairs. I waited, and waited... but never heard it hit the ground.

I shined my flashlight around the rest of the cave, trying to see if there was another path, but this was the only way forward. So I tested out the first step, glad when it held under my weight.

Then I began the long trek down.

# 43

# ANNIKA

I'd been going down the steps for what felt like hours. I wasn't sure exactly how much time had passed, but it was long enough that my stomach had started grumbling from the lack of food.

Finally, I saw something that I was starting to think I would never reach—the bottom.

I hurried down the last few steps, throwing my arms in the air in victory when my feet touched the ground. But I didn't want to waste time celebrating. Because ahead of me was a simple wooden door—it was the only object at the bottom of the stairs.

I reached forward to open it, surprised when it easily swung open. I sucked in a sharp breath as I gazed inside.

It was full of what appeared to be ancient, magical

objects. Crystals, swords, daggers, cards, pendants, jewelry… they were all there, covered in cobwebs, apparently having been undisturbed for decades.

There were also skeletons, laid out sporadically, their gaping eyes staring out at me and warning me to turn back around. My spine tingled under their hollow gazes, and I shuddered, unable to stop looking at them.

Who had these people been? Why hadn't they been able to escape?

I forced myself to avert my gaze, trying to shake the thoughts away. Those people were long dead.

There was only one thing I needed to worry about right now—finding that sapphire ring. It had to be in here somewhere. I just needed to find it and avoid touching any of the other objects in the process.

I approached a table surrounded by swords—on the table were pieces of jewelry. I ran my flashlight over each piece, making sure not to touch any of them.

It didn't take long to find the sapphire ring. After all, there weren't many pieces there, and only one of them was blue. But it was small, in a plain, simple setting. All of the other pieces were extravagant in comparison.

This *had* to be it.

I lifted it from the table, making sure to heed Camelia's advice and only touch the setting. The ring appeared to be in my size, and sure enough, it slipped easily onto my finger.

I held it out, admiring it. Although simple, the gem was truly beautiful, glistening as if it held a galaxy of stars within it. I'd never been super into jewelry, but wearing this ring somehow felt *right.*

Suddenly I heard something from up above—shrieks and flapping wings.

I tilted my flashlight up, screaming as a flock of bats shot straight down toward me.

# 44

## ANNIKA

THEY WERE IN MY FACE, in my hair—they were *everywhere*. I screamed and screamed, clawing at them to *get off*, but it didn't help.

I whipped the flashlight around, knocking as many of them in the head as possible, but soon they were on the flashlight, gripping it with their claws and pulling it from my grasp. They flung it somewhere far away, and it was so dark that I could barely see.

Still, they continued attacking, scratching at my skin and clawing at my clothes. I kept on screaming and swatting, but eventually fell down onto the ground, ready to give up.

They weren't stopping, and it *hurt*. I screamed at each tiny slice of my skin.

But was this really how I was going to meet my end? Not by a vampire, or wolves, or a witch... but by bats?

No. I refused to go down without a fight.

And so, despite Camelia's warning, I reached for one of the swords near the table and started swinging it blindly, trying to injure as many bats as possible.

Seconds after I started swinging, they stopped attacking. They flew back up to wherever they'd come from, and they were silent, as if they were never there at all.

I gripped the sword tighter, my heart racing at a million miles per minute. My skin burned where they'd attacked.

I hurried to where the flashlight had fallen and picked it up, still holding the sword with my other hand. After all, if the bats decided to attack again, I wanted to be ready.

Suddenly, the wooden door slammed shut, and the cave started to rumble. Quiet at first, and then louder and louder until the objects inside shook from the force. I could feel the rumbling deep in my chest. It sounded like an avalanche, and it pounded on the door, but somehow the door held strong.

I backed away, running to the end of the cave and holding my sword out ahead of me, as if that would be able to keep me safe from the crumbling cavern.

Finally, after minutes of shaking and rumbling, the

cave quieted. I looked around, but nothing seemed misplaced.

The rumbling seemed to have stopped for now.

I took another look at the glimmering ring on my finger. I'd gotten what I came here for—it was time to get out of here. But first, I placed the sword back down where I'd found it. Camelia had been explicit in her instructions—I wasn't to touch anything other than the ring. I didn't regret my actions—that sword had saved me from the bats—but these objects were full of powerful magic. Who knew what type of magic that sword contained?

A part of me wanted to bring it back with me in case I ran into another problem like the bats, but another part of me knew I shouldn't. Camelia had seemed confident that she could control the magic in the ring. And who knew what I would be letting loose with the sword? Best to leave it where it was.

And so, I made my way back towards the door, opened it... and my heart dropped at what I saw.

## 45

## ANNIKA

A PILE OF RUBBLE. That was all that was in front of me. The earthquake... the avalanche... the stairs must have broken apart and collapsed.

I had no way out of this cave.

I was stuck.

My chest tightened, and I looked around, searching for another way out. I ran around the room, placing my hands against the walls to search for an escape. A door, or *something*. The entire time, I avoided touching any of the magical objects. Because the stairs had collapsed immediately after I'd touched the sword.

Given Camelia's warning, I doubted that timing was a coincidence.

I pounded on the walls until my knuckles were raw and bleeding. But there were no secret doors. Eventually, I sunk down to the floor, defeated. It was no use. I was trapped here.

With no food or water, it wouldn't be long until I died. *If* I didn't run out of air and suffocate first.

I would deteriorate and join the skeletons decorating this haunted cavern.

This cave was cursed. I was stupid to have come in here to begin with.

If it hadn't been for those bats... I never would have needed to grab the sword. I would have been fine. I would have taken the ring, gone back up to Camelia, and been turned into a vampire.

I held out my hand, admiring the cursed ring that had brought me here in the first place. It truly was beautiful. How had a thing of such beauty caused me so much trouble? Soon I would be dead, and it was all the fault of this damned ring.

I twisted the ring off my finger, wanting to throw it across the room. But I stopped myself.

Because something else that Camelia had said flashed through my mind.

*The ring contains great power...*

She'd told me not to touch the stone, because I would release power that I wouldn't be able to control. But at this point, what did I have to lose?

If I touched the ring and found out what power it contained... well, I didn't know what would happen unless I tried. If I did nothing, I would surely die here.

And so, I reached for the ring, stroking it with my index finger. The sapphire was silky and smooth, and was it just my imagination, or did the stardust within brighten at my touch?

I pulled my finger away and looked closer. It wasn't my imagination. The sparkles of light were getting brighter and brighter, swirling around the gem. As if the ring had been brought to life. The swirling quickened, and then it rose from the gem completely.

It became a glowing orb in front of me, the shape morphing into the form of a beautiful young woman. She wasn't fully there—she was transparent, like a ghost—but her eyes met with mine and she smiled.

"Hello, Annika." Her voice was light, like an echo, bouncing off the walls of the cave. "It's a pleasure to finally meet you."

## 46

## ANNIKA

"Who are you?" I blinked a few times, making sure I wasn't imagining this.

Maybe the cave was running out of air and I was hallucinating? But she was still there. She was dressed in a vintage blue gown, and combined with her short, curled hair, she looked like a Hollywood starlet from the early twentieth century.

"*What* are you?" I continued. "And how do you know my name?"

"So many questions." She laughed, giving a small flick of her hand. "But it's fine. I'm happy to answer them all."

"Okay…" I watched her, waiting.

"My name is Geneva," she said simply. "And I am a witch."

"You don't look like a witch," I said, the image of Camelia popping into my mind. Camelia was solid and… alive. "You look like a ghost."

"I suppose I do, don't I?" She raised a hand in front of her eyes and looked through it, smiling sadly. "I appear this way because my kind turned against me. They cursed me. They created the curse just for me. They named it the 'genie curse.'" She laughed, although her laugh sounded hollow—defeated. "A play on my name. They thought it was clever." She reached out to touch the nearest object—a crystal ball of some sort—but her hand passed right through it. She snarled at her hand and let it fall back to her side. "I'm powerless to do anything for myself. I *feel* like a ghost. That's all I am —a ghost of who I used to be."

Questions raced through my mind—mainly if she could get me out of this cave—but demanding her to do something for me hardly seemed like a smart way to begin this relationship. So instead, I started with something else.

"Why did they curse you?" I asked, trying to swallow down the suspicion rising in my throat. Because Camelia had warned me that the objects in this cave were dangerous if not controlled by a witch who knew what she was doing. And if Geneva's kind had turned against her, I assumed they had a reason.

It was probably why Camelia had warned me against touching the gem.

"Jealousy," she said, her eyes darkening. "I was the most powerful witch in the world. The others were afraid of my powers. So, what do people do when they're afraid? Destroy the object of their fear. In their case—me."

"But they didn't destroy you," I said. "You're here."

"Barely." She huffed. "In case you didn't notice, I'm bound inside that ring on your finger. And my magic no longer belongs to me."

"What do you mean?" I asked. "Who does your magic belong to?"

She stared straight at me, her gaze sharp, and said, "My magic belongs to you."

## 47

## ANNIKA

"But I'm not a witch," I said. "I can't do magic."

She threw her head back and laughed. "Think for a second about what they named my curse," she said. "The *genie* curse. What do you know about genies, Annika?"

"You know my name," I realized again. "I never told you my name."

"I'm the most powerful witch in the world." She straightened. "I have strong psychic abilities. But back to the point—the curse. What do you know about genies?"

"Genies are trapped inside lamps," I said, and I held the ring out in front of me, everything clicking into place. "Or rings."

"Yes." She pressed her fingers together and leaned

forward. "Continue."

"I touched the ring—which I guess could be compared to rubbing a lamp—and you came out of it," I said. "And you said your magic belongs to me. So does that mean I get three wishes? Like if you were a genie?"

"Worse." Geneva frowned. "You see, my magic was so strong that the witches couldn't kill me. So they trapped me in that ring and locked it in this cursed cavern. They never expected anyone to be able to enter and retrieve it. They intended for the ring—and myself—to be lost forever. Because as long as my spirit is connected to the ring, I'm bound to serve its wearer for as long as the ring belongs to them."

"So you can get me out of this cavern." I smiled, relieved that for *once* since being kidnapped last year, things seemed to be working out in my favor. "You can teleport us out of here."

"I can." She nodded. "I can take you anywhere in the world."

Anywhere in the world? My mind raced with the possibilities. That was a huge offer.

The first place that came to mind was the Sanctuary that Jacen had mentioned—the place where humans could go and be free from all supernatural creatures.

But if I went there, what would happen to the ring? To Geneva? Surely she wouldn't be allowed inside the Sanctuary. And Jacen… he'd risked so much to help me escape. I hadn't seen him since Camelia and her guards had attacked us in the mountains. I didn't know if he was okay. He didn't know if *I* was okay.

Given all that he'd done for me, I *needed* to see him again.

And then there was Camelia. As much as I was wary of her, we'd made a blood oath. She'd promised to turn me into a vampire if I gave her the ring.

"What are you thinking, girl?" Geneva asked.

"I thought you were psychic," I said. "Shouldn't you *know* what I'm thinking?"

"It doesn't work like that," she said.

"Oh." I frowned. "Well, I was thinking about a lot of things. Mainly that I'm not sure where I would go. You see, the vampires of the Vale killed my family. And given all that I know of the supernatural world, I could never return to living a normal human life."

"Do you want me to wipe your memory of the knowledge of the supernatural?" she asked. "Because it's in my power to do so. And if you wish it, I can—"

"No!" I said sharply. "I don't want to forget. I won't be ignorant. I won't let myself be a victim ever again."

"Good." She smiled. "I was hoping you would say that."

"Also, I made a blood oath with Camelia," I told her. "She's the strongest witch of the Vale. She *has* to follow through with her promise to me."

"What did you promise her?" Geneva raised an eyebrow. "Because blood oaths are a strong, ancient magic—so strong that even I cannot reverse them."

"I promised her that I would give her the ring, and she promised that in return she would try her hardest to convince Queen Laila to turn me into a vampire."

"Those were the exact words?" Geneva asked.

"I think." I scratched my head, trying to recall the conversation we'd had in the dungeons. I still hadn't recovered from the vampire blood hangover at that point, so my memories were hazy. "I suppose I don't remember the *exact* wording. But it was close."

"Well, luckily you have me on your side." Geneva reached for the crystal nearby, but her hand passed through it again. "Rhatz!" she cursed, turning back to me. "I can't interact with anything in the mortal world unless you command me to do so."

"What were you trying to do?" I asked.

"I was going to use the crystal to view the moment when you made the blood oath with this witch Camelia," she said.

"Okay." I nodded. "Then I command you to use the crystal to view the moment I made the blood oath with Camelia."

Geneva reached for the crystal again, and this time, she was able to touch it. She grinned and pulled the crystal onto her lap, her hands hovering above it as she gazed inside.

"Well?" I asked, leaning forward. "What do you see?"

She looked up at me and smiled. "I saw the moment you made the oath with Camelia," she said. "She promised that *if* you gave her the sapphire ring, she would tell Queen Laila of your feat and do everything in her power to convince her to turn you into a vampire."

"If," I realized. "Not when."

"Exactly." Geneva smirked. "You're under no oath to give my ring to this witch Camelia. In fact, I urge you not to do so. This witch never had your best intentions at heart."

"What do you mean?" I asked. "She swore that she would do everything in her power to turn me into a vampire."

"She also told everyone in the palace that you were dead," Geneva said simply. "Including your vampire prince Jacen."

"No." I shook my head, my heart dropping deep into my stomach. "She wouldn't."

"She would," Geneva said.

"Even if she did, he wouldn't believe it," I insisted. "Not without seeing a body."

"Your instincts are correct," Geneva said. "While you were sedated, Camelia stole a strand of your hair and created a transformation potion. She gave the potion to your friend Tanya—the short blonde girl who worked at that bar with you. Once Tanya had taken on your form, Camelia had her killed. She showed the girl in your form as proof of your demise."

I shook my head, unwilling to so easily accept that Tanya was gone. "That doesn't make any sense." I reached for the crystal, but Geneva pulled it away.

"Do *not* touch that." She held it out of my reach, her eyes ablaze.

"Why not?" I asked.

"Because as long as you wear my ring, it's my duty to protect you," she said. "And the dark crystals contain powerful magic that kills non-witches on contact."

"Oh." I flexed my fingers, shocked that I'd just been millimeters away from death—and grateful to Geneva for saving me. "Thank you."

"No need to thank me," she said. "If a wearer of the ring dies on my watch, I'll be trapped in its depths until the end of time. I will always save its wearer. Anything else would mean condemning myself to an eternity of imprisonment."

I wanted to point out how selfish that sounded, but I kept my mouth shut. Because she was my only hope —*and* she was apparently bound to do as I said and keep me alive—so I had to make sure this relationship got off on the right footing.

"Tanya's truly dead?" I asked instead, my voice cracking.

"Yes," she said. "I'm sorry for your loss."

I didn't respond to her empty condolences. Geneva didn't care about my grief. In fact, I had an instinctive feeling that all Geneva cared about was herself.

Luckily, Geneva's self was tied to my self. And I wanted revenge. On Camelia, for killing Mike and Tanya. On Laila, for creating this kingdom that treated humans like animals. On all the vampire nobles who followed her blindly, enjoying their lives in the palace while we lived in poverty. And on the vampire guards who had killed my family, along with countless other innocent lives.

And I had the most powerful witch in the world at my disposal to help me do so.

I would *not* let this opportunity go to waste.

"I should go to Jacen," I realized, running my hands through my hair. "He'll help me figure out what to do from here."

"Are you so sure about him?" Geneva asked with a knowing smile.

"Yes," I said firmly. "He tried to save my life. He'll help me. I *know* he will."

She placed the crystal down between us, watching me carefully. "When I looked for the moment when you made the blood oath with Camelia, I saw something else as well," she said. "Something that I think you'll want to see."

"Show me," I told her. "I command it."

Then she held her hands above the crystal and showed me Jacen's heartless reaction when he'd learned of my death.

# 48

# ANNIKA

"No." I shook my head, blinking away a tear as I watched his reaction for the second time. "He couldn't have meant it."

"Vampires are cold, selfish creatures," Geneva said sharply. "Usually it takes over a century for them to lose touch with their humanity, but others give in more easily." She gestured toward Jacen, as if referring to him.

I watched the scene once more, searching for a sign that Jacen cared. But I found none. Instead, my heart broke again as I watched him say that he cared nothing for me. That he was bored and I was a toy.

That it likely wouldn't have been long until he tired of me and drained me dry.

He was so cold and emotionless. So unlike the

person I'd believed him to be when we met in the village square.

"There's still one thing that doesn't make sense," I said, wiping the tears from my cheeks. "Why would Camelia make the oath to do everything possible to turn me into a vampire and then go to such measures to make everyone think I was dead?"

"There are many ways around a blood oath." Geneva pressed the pads of her fingers together, appearing deep in thought. "Camelia never spoke her intentions out loud, and I cannot read her thoughts, but as a fellow witch I *can* tell you what I might do in her position if she truly wanted you dead."

"Go on," I said, needing to hear it.

"She could ask Laila to turn you into a vampire, and once the transformation was complete, she could kill you."

"She wouldn't." I gasped.

"She would." Geneva leaned forward, as if daring me to contradict her. "I saw a lot when I gazed into the crystal. I learned that Camelia is desperate for immortality—she wants to become a vampire. Laila promised she would turn her if she found a witch powerful enough to be her replacement."

"Which was why she was so intent on finding your ring," I realized. "And using me to get what she wanted."

"Exactly," Geneva said. "Perhaps you're not as dimwitted as I initially thought."

"I'm not dimwitted." I crossed my arms and glared at her. "It's just… this is a lot to take in at once."

"For a human, I suppose it would be," she said, brushing me off the same way all the supernaturals seemed to do. "And I assume you're going to have many questions. So before we discuss what you want from me, I should explain my limitations."

"I thought you were the most powerful witch in the world," I said, my tone dripping with sarcasm. "Surely you have no limitations?"

"Everyone has limitations." She rolled her eyes. "Even the angels themselves. Now, do you want to hear what mine are, or not?" She studied her nails, as if she had better places to be, and glanced back up at me, waiting.

"Of course I do." I leaned back against the wall, making myself comfortable. "Go ahead."

"Thank you." She cleared her throat, straightening her shoulders. "First of all, I can't communicate with or bring back the dead," she started, and my heart dropped at the bomb that I couldn't bring back my parents, my brother, Mike, or Tanya. "Don't look so disappointed." She sneered. "A million people would kill to wear that ring on your finger."

I twisted the ring, gazing down at it sadly. She might

be right, but it didn't stop me from missing my family and friends.

Still, I got a hold of myself, refocusing on the conversation at hand.

"Is that your only limitation?" I asked.

"No," she said. "But I don't have many, so this won't take much longer."

I motioned for her to continue.

"Along with not being able to raise the dead, I also can't kill anyone," she said. "At least, not with magic."

"Have you ever killed anyone *without* magic?" I asked.

"That's none of your concern." She waved away my question. "Especially since I can't interact with the mortal world, and you only have command of my *magic*. So even if I wanted to kill someone without magic, I wouldn't be able to do so. I could use my magic to get you in the position to kill someone, but the killing would be on you."

"Good to know." I nodded, feeling more and more suspicious of her by the second. With everything she said, I worried that the witches truly *did* have good reasons for locking her away forever.

But now, she was on my side. I couldn't let myself forget that, no matter *what* other crazy things she might say. And she was right that a million people would kill to have possession of this ring.

I wouldn't let my luck go to waste.

"I can't manipulate or travel through time," she continued. "And lastly, I can't make anyone fall in love. Love potions and spells—as fascinating as they would be—are things of mythology. They don't exist."

"I wouldn't have anyone to use one on, anyway," I muttered.

"Not even your handsome, silver-eyed prince?" She smirked.

My heart broke at the mere mention of Jacen. "He hates me." I tried to sound as cold as he'd sounded when he'd said he was toying with me and would eventually kill me, but my voice wavered, giving away how much he'd hurt me.

"Perhaps," Geneva said. "But men are fickle creatures. Totally untrustworthy, if you ask me."

"Bad experience?" I asked.

"I was the most powerful witch in the world," she reminded me for the gazillionth time. "Men don't like women who are stronger than they are. It *emasculates* them." She crossed her arms, and I couldn't help smiling slightly, proud of myself for hitting a nerve in her seemingly icy interior.

But of course, she recovered nearly immediately.

"Now you know my limitations, and you know the truth about those you thought you trusted," she continued. "So tell me, young mortal… what do you wish for?"

# 49

# ANNIKA

I PRESSED MY LIPS TOGETHER, contemplating her question.

What did I wish for?

My two closest friends were gone. My family was gone. My grandparents had been dead for years, and both of my parents had been only siblings. So I didn't have any extended family who might want to care for me. And even if I did, I could never go back to living a normal life. Not after everything I now knew existed.

I wrapped my arms around myself, my chest feeling hollow, and it hurt to breathe. Because there was no one left who cared about me. No one left who *loved* me.

I was alone in the world.

My thoughts wandered to Jacen—to the person I thought he'd been when he was trying to help me escape. During the time we'd been together, I'd actually let myself *feel* something for him. I'd thought he'd felt something for me, too. But I was being desperate and foolish. Pinning any bit of hope on a person I'd just met. A person who apparently had eventually planned on murdering me.

I wouldn't make that mistake again.

So what did I want right now?

I wanted revenge.

Revenge on the vampires of the Vale—all of them. They'd ruined my life in every possible way. And not just my life. They'd ruined *countless* lives. They needed to be stopped. The humans who were trapped in the village needed to be freed.

I wanted to destroy the Vale… but how? It was so carefully guarded, not just by vampires, but by wolves. The vampires never let anyone inside the palace except for their own.

Even Geneva's magic couldn't possibly save me from an entire kingdom of supernaturals set on destroying me.

But then I smiled, remembering the rest of the conversation Jacen had had with Laila after telling her he would have drained me dry. Specifically the part where he'd said he was going to welcome vampires from across the world inside the palace.

*That* was my way inside the palace—as a contender for his hand in marriage.

It was the only way to get close enough to all of them and remain undetected so I could figure out a way to destroy them.

"You look like you have an idea." Geneva rubbed her hands together, clearly ready to get started. "Please, do tell."

"I want you to turn me into a vampire." I stared her straight in the eyes, wanting her to have no doubt about my conviction. "And not just any vampire. I wish to be a vampire princess."

# FROM THE AUTHOR

I hope you enjoyed The Vampire Wish! If so, I'd love if you left a review. Reviews help readers find the book, and I read each and every one of them.

There are five books in the Vampire Wish series. The next is The Vampire Prince, and you can turn the page to check out the description.

Enjoy!

## THE VAMPIRE PRINCE

**To *destroy* the enemy, she will *become* the enemy.**

Everything has been taken from Annika — her family, her friends, and even her freedom — by the vampires who enslaved her in the hidden kingdom of the Vale. But now she possesses a magical ring that contains Geneva, the most powerful witch in the world, and she's ready for revenge.

When Prince Jacen invites vampire princesses from all over the world to the palace to compete for his hand in marriage, Annika finds her chance. By commanding Geneva to turn her into a vampire princess, she can try to win the cold heart of the prince who betrayed her and left her for dead.

Can she keep the emotions she used to feel for Jacen in check? Because if her deception works and she becomes his bride, she'll have full access to the palace... and she can destroy the Vale from the inside.

But with powerful players vying for control of the ring, and a dark magic rising outside the kingdom, there's far more at stake than just the crown.

**Return to the magical world of the Vale in the second book of The Vampire Wish series and get ready for twists and turns that you'll never see coming!**

## ABOUT THE AUTHOR

Michelle Madow is a *USA Today* bestselling author of fast-paced fantasy novels that will leave you turning the pages wanting more! Her books are full of magic, adventure, romance, and twists you'll never see coming.

Michelle grew up in Maryland, and now lives in Florida. She's loved reading for as long as she can remember. She wrote her first book in her junior year of college and hasn't stopped writing since! She also loves traveling, and has been to all seven continents. Someday, she hopes to travel the world for a year on a cruise ship.

**Never miss a new release by signing up to get emails or texts when Michelle's books come out:**

**Sign up for emails:** michellemadow.com/subscribe
**Sign up for texts:** michellemadow.com/texts

**Connect with Michelle:**

**Facebook Group:** facebook.com/groups/michellemadow
**Instagram:** @michellemadow
**Email:** michelle@madow.com
**Website:** www.michellemadow.com

Printed in Poland
by Amazon Fulfillment
Poland Sp. z o.o., Wrocław
10 March 2022

c1448ade-b9a3-48aa-8403-09ce9b786fb6R01